W9-CMJ-918

ST. MARTIN'S

MINOTAUR

MYSTERIES

Other titles from St. Martin's **Minotaur** Mysteries

St. Martin's Paperbacks is also proud to present
these mystery classics by Ngaio Marsh

"FOUL PLAY?"

Roy Gross, [campus Chief of Security], was a tall, meatless man with a prominent nose and eyes that seemed to be looking for the lenses of his glasses rather than through them. He grunted when Phil came to a stop beside him and looked down at the lifeless body of the young woman the paramedics had removed from the water.

"Foul play?"

"She was found face down in the water, but how she died is unclear."

Clarity would come when the medical examiner arrived. The paramedics—the female with a crew cut, the male with a luxuriant ponytail—had sought to revive the woman but unsuccessfully.

"Water in her lungs?"

A shake of the head.

"So she didn't drown."

"I didn't say that." Caution brimmed in the ponytail's eyes, which then went up the hill to where the ME's vehicle had come into view.

Father Carmody went down to join Phil but Roger remained above, looking out at the lake like a ship in dry dock longing for the wash of waves against his side. "Beautiful!" Roger sighed.

He referred to the snow that had continued its immaculate slow descent during the grim proceedings by the lakeshore. The waters of the lake were dark and metallic, stirred by the slight breeze that brought snow in at an angle . . . It had still not struck Roger that the object lying down there on the shore of the lake was the mortal remains of Amanda Pick . . .

St. Martin's Paperbacks Titles
by Ralph McInerny

The Mysteries at the University of
Notre Dame Series:

On This Rockne
Lack of the Irish
Irish Tenure

IRISH TENURE

RALPH McINERNY

St. Martin's Paperbacks

IRISH TENURE

Copyright © 1999 by Ralph McInerny.
Excerpt from *The Book of Kills* copyright © 2000 by Ralph McInerny.

All rights reserved. No part of this book may be used or reproduced in any manner whatsoever without written permission except in the case of brief quotations embodied in critical articles or reviews. For information address St. Martin's Press, 175 Fifth Avenue, New York, N.Y. 10010.

Library of Congress Catalog Card Number: 99-16992

ISBN: 0-312-97320-9

Printed in the United States of America

St. Martin's Press hardcover edition / December 1999
St. Martin's Paperbacks edition / September 2000

10   9   8   7   6   5   4   3   2   1

I have seen, where a strange country
Opened its secret plains about me,
One great Golden Dome stand lonely with its
golden image, one
Seen afar, in strange fulfillment,
Through the sunlit Indian Summer
That Apocalyptic portent that has clothed her
with the Sun.

—G. K Chesterton

PROLOGUE
DECEMBER

THE BODY WAS DISCOVERED IN one of the lakes on campus by Blanche Crowley, a retired member of the Saint Mary's faculty, who was seventy-three and hoped to live at least a decade more. To this end she ate sensibly, smoked only when no witnesses were present, and every morning jogged along the path encircling the campus lakes, going around twice before heading for breakfast with Emily House, who preferred indoor exercise at the Loftus Center.

The winter scene that morning might have recalled the historic date when Fr. Edward Sorin and his companions arrived to take possession of this land, calling it Notre Dame du Lac, but the temperature had risen over the past twenty-four hours, causing a thaw. Now, in the morning chill, the path was glazed and this dictated deliberate and sure-footed progress. Blanche ran with the ritualistic dedication of the regular jogger, bringing each arthritic knee up almost to chin level and lowering her gaudy white jogging shoes with practiced care.

The first time Blanche passed the point where the path ran below Holy Cross House she noticed something in the shallow water offshore but thought it was discarded clothing. An odd thought, but then she was exercising and her brain was bounced about as she ran, making mental clarity elusive. Coming around the second time, grateful for the interruption, Blanche stopped running and looked more closely.

It was indeed clothing in the water, female clothing. Blanche edged closer, then stopped. With sudden horror she realized that there was someone in the clothing, half submerged in the lake. She danced back, her eyes wild and her mouth agape. But no noise emerged until she was twenty-five feet farther along the path. By the time she got to the boathouse her screaming became audible and could be heard for a radius of a hundred yards.

PART ONE

BEFORE

1

ing the night and now lay like a benediction on the campus.
Trees were festooned with it, the ledges of windows bore its gra-
cious burden, tile roofs were rendered more colorful by the
addition of traces of white, the shrubbery seemed decorated.
And at the grotto, the kneeling Bernadette wore a cap of snow.

Rising students went to their windows and responded to the
scene in ways calculated to conceal their delight. Groans, trite
remarks about South Bend weather, the lament that fall was
over and winter upon them, all these were heard. But in truth
hearts thrilled to the sign that one season was gone and the end
of the semester was in sight.

Plows raced over the sidewalks, clearing the way for students to get to dining halls and classrooms.

In residence hall chapels, mass was being said. It would be
offered in one chapel or another, and in Sacred Heart Basilica,
at intervals throughout the day. The growing Muslim population
in married student housing raised their voices in prescribed
prayer. Soon the droning voices of professors would be heard in
the classrooms and labs of the campus.

Notre Dame is a city of ten thousand souls, whose undergraduate population turns over completely every four years.
(And not, as Prof. Sean Pottery has said, in order to go to sleep
again.) Each year there is an influx of new faces, the swaggering
confidence of those starting a second or third year, and the
excited unease of seniors for whom their final year suddenly
looms like ejection from the Garden of Eden. But they have no

reason for fear. When they are gone, the portal of return will be in the custody of the Notre Dame Alumni Association, not the angels of exclusion, and generous hearts will always be welcomed back by their alma mater. In a distant future, however toothless and forgetful they become, they will always remember that they are Domers who spent the best years of their youth at Our Lady's University.

The faculty, a more stable element, numerically, is divided, not quite as sheep and goats, but rather into the tenured and the untenured. The first six years as a member of the faculty are probationary, though one's appointment must be renewed after three years. Then there looms the single greatest crisis in the academic life, the tenure decision. There are minimal generic conditions for tenure that the tyro can find in the faculty manual, but it is more important to see the interpretation of those rules in his or her home department. The abstract and impersonal tribunal translates into flesh and blood colleagues, whose fateful function it is to apply the rules to given cases. A departmental committee is elected and assigned the task of scouting the terrain for new additions to the faculty and, more importantly, of deciding who shall pass from the tentative ranks of the untenured into the security and peace of lifetime employment. Members of this committee are understandably objects of unwonted deference from the young; they are viewed warily, their *obiter dicta* and facial expressions subjected to lengthy meditation during sleepless nights. No wonder. To have tenure on any faculty is bliss, but to be a tenured member of the Notre Dame faculty is very heaven.

Horace Cheval and Bridget Quirk, senior members of the philosophy department and the guiding voices of the tenure and promotion committee, met this wintry morning in the departmental mail room in O'Shaughnessy. Wordlessly, they exchanged manila envelopes. From Cheval to Bridget went the information on which the fate of Hans Wiener depended. From Bridget to Cheval went Amanda Pick's dossier. The fate of these two young people would be decided by the committee on which Cheval and Quirk sat. Old hands at academic give-and-take, the two were practiced in not giving the other a hint of any preliminary judgments they might have formed about the two candidates for tenure.

"Such a beautiful snow," Bridget said. She hated snow but somehow she felt safer in this brighter world.

"A damned nuisance," Cheval replied.

"This is dreadful coffee."

"I am drinking tea."

Cheval was ready to head off at all costs any recounting of the most memorable event in Bridget Quirk's lengthy stay at Notre Dame. Bridget exercised along the path that had once been a railroad bed and which, transformed, now enabled one to walk from Saint Mary's to the river and along it to the trace, even to Howard Park for those with stamina. Bridget had been one of these, her exercise the kind of walking that involves the hips to a disjointed degree, the upper body all but immobile. Thus she would strut and fret along the walk of a late afternoon, seeking to stave off the inevitable debilities of age. A year ago, to her horrified amazement, one murky twilit afternoon she had been pounced upon from behind. The belly purse she wore was torn from her, and Bridget was wondering wildly if there really are fates worse than death when her attacker abandoned her.

"He must have heard someone coming." She shuddered at the nearness of her escape.

"Did someone come along?"

Actually, abandoned by her would-be ravisher, Bridget had run full steam to LaSalle Avenue where she attempted to stop traffic, a wild woman in a jogging costume, flailing her arms as she stood in the middle of the road.

"A mugging," Cheval had concluded.

"In the event," Bridget retorted. It was important for her to see herself as a survivor of an unsuccessful rape. She lectured women students on how to handle themselves in such a situation, she put new life into the escort service for women on cam-

7

pus, with Laura Flynn she founded Women of the University of Notre Dame and had refused to alter the name of the organization when it was pointed out the acronym it formed. Including every word gave WOTUOND, which suggested a Nordic deity or, worse, rotund in baby talk. They were determined to have WOUND. Rather than apologize for its implications, Bridget and her sisters flaunted it. But only Bridget and Laura Flynn had gone to the extreme of having it emblazoned in large letters on the backs of the jackets they wore when exercising. Memorable, no doubt, but not catching; other members confined their solidarity to moral support. Dozens of unsold jackets in various sizes took up space in the Office of the Counselor for Student Complaints, run by Jewel Fondue.

"I don't suppose it was meant to be more serious," Cheval had mused after the attack on Bridget.

"More serious than attempted rape? What do you mean?"

"My surmise is too fanciful."

"Tell me." Bridget's tone drew a line in the conversational sand.

"A preemptive strike. Someone who is coming up for tenure wanted to take you out."

"Take me out!"

"A *façon de parler.* Kill you."

Bridget yelped in alarm, but then she saw the ironic glint in Cheval's eye and turned her yelp to laughter, ever the good soldier. With time her references to her struggle on the jogging path grew less frequent though not less vivid. But she had learned to expect no sympathy from Horace Cheval who was, after all, a male.

Bridget now looked thoughtful, as if his reference to tenure decisions had brought her back to the present. "What are your views on Chesterton?"

"I have none." He squinted at her. Was this some reference to their common task? It was their custom to refer to it only in a coded, noncommittal way. He wrinkled his nose at his tea.

8

Others came into the mail room and Quirk and Cheval gave way.

"You might ask Sean Pottery in English," Horace said, when they were in the hall.

"Ask him what?"

"About Chesterton."

"Ah."

2

great writer to fall into the hands of fans and afficionados. Thus it is that one can find on library shelves the *Joyce Newsletter*, the *Faulkner Flyer*, *Trollope Notes*, the *Oates Bag*, *Wolfe Call*, *What's Updike?* and all the rest. There was no good reason to think that Gilbert Keith Chesterton would be spared this scholarly *osculum mortis*, but that did not mean the outrage would go unnoticed, certainly not by Sean Pottery.

"Look at this," he exclaimed, fluttering the leaves of a rather expensive-looking publication. He had bustled into the faculty lounge and collapsed into the chair next to Roger Knight's.

"It seems well done," Roger replied.

"Overdone, my dear fellow. Cooked to a crisp. Sycophancy of the worst kind."

Pottery taught a course on Chesterton and was universally acknowledged as the expert on the Father Brown stories. In the manner peculiar to scholars he had developed a proprietary air toward the object of his research and sought to fend off fans rather than attract them. Others writing on Chesterton had the look of poachers to him, and he was in principle prepared to be unimpressed by anyone else's interpretation of *his* author. His enemies suggested that Pottery would have regarded the living Chesterton himself as a rival.

"Didn't Chesterton spend time at Notre Dame, Sean?" Roger asked, knowing the answer, but deferring to the massive ego of his colleague.

"Shhh. Good Lord, if that got out!"

"Out? I should think you would be proud of the association."

"It is not my own reaction I was thinking of."

"Of course."

Roger had been told of Pottery's eccentricities and his perhaps pardonable desire to have his subject to himself, chasing off all others. For all that, Pottery was an entertaining and learned man, whose thirty years on the faculty of the University of Notre Dame had had a notable local effect. He was a legendary lecturer, one of the last of the classroom curmudgeons.

"Write it down!" he would shout at an indolent student. "Take notes! I will not waste my sweetness on the desert air!"

Some students dropped his course after one encounter, but others braved his wrath in order to enjoy the pure theater of his performance. Roger had slipped into the back of the lecture hall once to get the flavor of the man and regretted that there had been no one like him when he was an undergraduate at Princeton. Pottery spoke of literature as if he owned it, though the only public claim he had staked was the Father Brown stories of Chesterton. As for Chesterton's visit to Notre Dame in the early 1930s, despite his fear that knowledge of it might fall into the wrong hands, an account of that glorious occasion was part of what Pottery referred to as his standard repertoire.

"Were you a student here at the time?" Roger asked.

The famed Pottery brows rose above the dark plastic circles of his glasses. "I am not as old as you seem to think. Nor am I an alumnus of this institution."

"It's hard to imagine you anywhere else."

"Imagination has nothing to do with it. It is a simple fact that I attended the College of Saint Alcuin."

Roger kept silent for a moment. "I don't think I know it."

"It no longer exists. I will not say that, having fulfilled its function in educating me, it ceased to be. Actually it hung on for some decades before succumbing to what was called 'the quest of excellence.'"

"There must be some still alive who remember Chesterton's visit."

Pottery found this possibility uninteresting. For him, Chesterton was an author of essays and stories and novels and books on a variety of topics. He existed on the written page. That he had actually trod the same ground as Pottery, had lectured to enthusiastic groups of students in Washington Hall, was an historical fact, not a personal memory.

"Writers were not meant to be the objects of personal adulation, the object of fan clubs. I have met admirers of Hemingway who have read nothing he wrote but dote on bullfights."

"And Chestertonians who merely like to drink?"

Too late Roger remembered that Pottery had, in his own description, an immoderate love of the grape, a fact attested to by his veined and rosy nose.

In medio stat virtus. Neither a lush nor a teetotaler be, as Shakespeare did not say. . . . "

"It is pleasant to think of Chesterton on this campus."

"You'll find an excellent account in Maisie Ward's biography."

"Maisie Ward's *Chesterton!*" Tom Stritch boomed from across the room. "Such a book. I read it just before I went into the navy. How it brought back those years."

"You remember when Chesterton lectured here?" Roger asked Stritch.

"My dear fellow, I will never forget it. It was the high point of my undergraduate years."

Roger managed to get to his feet and moved across the lounge to where Stritch, one of the emeriti, was enthroned.

"Have you ever told Pottery about it?"

"Pottery?"

It was Stritch's affectation not to know those he considered junior members of the faculty. There was the sound of a door slamming, and Roger turned to see that Professor Pottery had left the lounge. Roger introduced himself, mentioning that Father

Carmody had promised to make sure Roger met the diminutive professor whose voice had the carry of a male Ethel Merman.

"Ah, Carmody. And what brings you to campus?"

"Father Carmody was instrumental in getting me a faculty appointment."

"You sound grateful, as well perhaps you might be. There is a passage in Plato where those saved from shipwreck thank their rescuer." Stritch paused and fixed Roger with his eye. "The philosopher wonders what future perils he may have saved them for."

"In what dialogue is that found?"

Stritch ignored the question. "Who was that fellow who left?"

"Professor Pottery. He has been on the faculty for more than a quarter of a century. Father Carmody told me that he is a worthy successor to you and Frank O'Malley."

"And Dick Sullivan, John Frederick, Yves Simon, Joe Evans, Bob Fitzsimons . . . "

Stritch might have gone on calling the roll of the great Notre Dame dons. Still, he considered the list finite, indeed finished, no further additions being possible. It was his theory that the introduction of graduate studies had been the death of the university. The faculty no longer saw as their central and essential task addressing the living young people seated in the classroom before them. Now they sought reputations elsewhere in their field, they went off to meetings and conferences, they published things meant to be read by experts. Unjust as the judgment was, Sean Pottery was a symbol of all that Tom Stritch disliked and Roger knew better than to defend him. That Pottery and Stritch chose to be strangers to one another somehow made friendship with each more desirable to Roger.

One of the unexpected turns in Pottery's life was his infatuation with Amanda Pick, a half-agonized, half-amused account of which Roger had been given by the assistant professor of philosophy herself, whom he had met in the archives and with whom he had become friendly. She had acquired visibility for Pottery when she stopped by his office the previous April to advise him that she had come upon a rather good copy of *The Coloured Lands* in a Chicago used bookstore. His hand went to his heart and he fell back in his chair, closing his eyes. *"Nunc dimittis servum tuum, domine."* He opened his eyes. "I suppose they are asking a fortune for it."

"I don't think the owner had any idea of its value."

"It could not be had for a thousand pounds in England."

She took the book from her briefcase and handed it to him. "He let me have it for five dollars. Would you like to have it?"

No sinner could have been more grateful for a plenary indulgence on his death bed. Pottery took the book gingerly, placed it on his desk, and for a moment tears stood in his eyes. "All my life . . . " he began, but he could not go on.

The gift had been wholly disinterested. Roger Knight had told Amanda of Sean Pottery's scholarly interest and that had popped into her mind when she saw the book in Chicago. She would have assumed he already owned it, and when his reaction made it clear that he did not, she impulsively offered it to him.

In subsequent weeks, gratitude turned to friendship. He took her to dinner; he shared his table in the bar of the Morris Inn with her. There he was wont to hold court from sundown to some ungodly hour, regaling students, debating present and absent colleagues, fulminating on this and that, bringing his blood alcohol level slowly to capacity. He left in a taxi, driven off to his bachelor apartment. His undergraduate college had been all male, he had joined the Notre Dame faculty before coeducation, he had never taken female students or colleagues with complete seriousness. He was prepared to patronize Amanda, even as he let her know how truly grateful for her gift he was. She surprised him. At the time, she knew only two works of Chesterton, *Orthodoxy* and *The Everlasting Man*, and much preferred the second.

"*Orthodoxy* is considered his masterpiece."

"Don't you think it's a little cute?"

" 'Cute.' " That should have been the end of it. He had thanked her fulsomely, he would always be grateful for her gift, but such heresy was not to be tolerated. However, she went on about part one of *The Everlasting Man* and said things well worth attending to. Pottery's annoyance at her description of *Orthodoxy* receded. Although she would take nothing but a single glass of sweet vermouth, neat, no ice, he found her company delightful. Astrik Gabriel had once warned him never to trust a man who doesn't drink. Perhaps women were an exception to that sensible rule. He liked the way she made him justify his opinions. For too long he had been allowed to pontificate. She added a dimension to the evening that had always been absent from his life; he found it oddly stimulating to be disagreed with.

Amanda would not make a habit of spending the evening in the bar of the Morris Inn, and summer intervened in any case, but they became friends. With the resumption of classes in the fall, they began to see one another regularly again. Pottery found himself looking forward to their times together. Of course they spoke of the impending tenure decision.

Pottery invited Cheval to lunch in the University Club and asked how Amanda's prospects looked. The professor of philosophy lifted his milky eyes. "Bridget is on the committee."

"Bridget?"

"Bridget Quirk."

Pottery asked her to lunch in the Morris Inn. Conversations with Amanda had led him to be confident that he understood the female soul. He told Professor Quirk that he knew a young colleague of hers.

"Amanda Pick," Professor Quirk repeated. "She is up for tenure this year."

"How does it look for her?"

"Do you know Horace Cheval?"

"He's on the committee?"

She nodded and rolled her eyes, her manner suggesting that Cheval was all that stood between Amanda and permanence at Notre Dame. His lunch with Cheval had reassured Pottery about him; apparently Quirk was no obstacle. No need to tell Amanda of these inquiries, but he conveyed to her that he understood her prospects were bright.

It was a mark of Pottery's infatuation that he welcomed the news that Amanda was at work on an article dealing with Chesterton's visit to Notre Dame. He told her what he knew; he urged her to consult the archives. "That place is full of undiscovered treasures."

3

rare books by a fluke.

Nowadays he spoke of the store in Saint Louis as something he had inherited from his father, but the truth was that the book business, like every other practical endeavor, had defeated his father. The store had been rented and the books, already crated and stored when the owner had refused to continue the lease after half a year of delinquency in rent payments, drew little more than a sniff from the auctioneer. By that time Noah had given up any hope of raising enough from the sale to pay off the debts his father owed. The fact that storage rent was owed on the books was the main reason Noah inherited anything at all— in the event, his heritage consisted of half a year's rent due to the storage company and the crates of books.

It had been the interest of a girl he was going with at the time that had prompted Noah to take on the obligation and the books. Her name had been Rebecca and she professed to have a passion for books. When they spent an afternoon in the warehouse checking out the contents, Noah was surprised by his own reaction as he held in his hand old books whose authors were then unknown to him. But he had the eerie sense that his fingers were actually touching the past. He was hooked. Rebecca, it turned out, had thought the books would be new, or at least recently published books, and the dusty, yellowing treasure that Noah had inherited failed to captivate her.

In the days that followed, Noah found that he no longer wished to excel at Otis, Otis and Levitt, the law firm that had hitherto seemed to him, as it continued to seem to Rebecca, the earthly equivalent of nirvana. Ambition to flourish in the law had blown away like a wisp. Noah rented a store, moved the stock he had inherited into it, and for seven years enjoyed a life first of penury, then of breaking even, until eventually he began to make a modest living. But the main bonus was to spend his days among his books, acquiring new ones, reluctantly letting some go to customers.

The fateful step into affluence had come when he had joined a clearing house for used book dealers with a web site. Once his stock became part of that data base, his business experienced a quantum jump. Now with a potentially national clientele, he discovered that anything connected with Notre Dame attracted buyers. That was why he bid for and won the books and papers of Henry Horan, rightly suspecting that it would contain Notre Dame memorabilia.

Horan had played football in the early 1930s and then gone on to medical school. Several of his medical patents made him wealthy. Given his background, given the fact that he was a legendary Domer, as alumni were called, it might have been expected that he would be a generous benefactor of his alma mater. But he'd had a falling-out with the administration, actually refused election to the board of trustees, and in the end made only a modest contribution of papers to the University of Notre Dame Archives. Noah's hunch that there would be other valuable things remaining in Horan's papers was not wrong, but the most tantalizing find was one that he could not profit from.

The revelation had come in the diary Horan had kept in 1930 when he was a junior and on the staff of *Scholastic Magazine*. Like the student body generally, Horan had been enthralled by the presence on campus of the famous English writer Gilbert Keith Chesterton. He had attended every lecture. He had taken down every word of the series on the Victorian Age in Literature, using the same self-devised shorthand found in the diaries and which Noah had finally managed to decode.

The entries detailing the great revelation were both coded and enigmatic. A bold lad, Horan had approached Chesterton and asked for an original contribution to the *Scholastic*. The great man had already composed the poem about Notre Dame football. Horan told him he was thinking of a Father Brown story. It had been some years since Chesterton had written a Father Brown story. Horan had approached Chesterton when the writer was *in medio jubilationis*, meaning, Noah surmised, drunk. Chesterton agreed. More surprisingly he remembered the promise and several days later gave Horan the story. The reason it had never appeared in the *Scholastic* was that Horan had kept the transaction a secret. No one else on the staff knew of the story. Meanwhile, Chesterton's sojourn ended, he departed, and Horan was left with the holograph version of a hitherto unpublished Chesterton story and a conscience that would give him no rest.

References to the story became less frequent with the passage of time, but the anguish with which Horan referred to the purloined story did not lessen. For he had no doubt that the story was stolen. Yes, it was his idea to ask Chesterton for the story. Yes, the story had been given to him. He tried to convince himself that Chesterton's understanding of the nature of the promise was so hazy that it might be interpreted as a personal promise to Horan. The young man tried every dodge of the guilty conscience, but he was never able to see himself as other than a thief. Of course he confessed the fault. His confessor had difficulty understanding the problem and in any case thought it a less than serious matter. He gave Horan absolution but afterward Horan sat in a pew staring at the sanctuary, certain that he was unshriven. A month later he took the matter to a more knowledgeable confessor.

"Publish it," was the cryptic advice.

"Father?"

"Print it in the *Scholastic* and put an end to the matter."

That was the entry that prompted Noah to write the Notre

21

Dame archives to ask for the tables of contents of the *Scholastic* over the relevant two-year period. The story had never appeared.

It seemed clear that Horan's conscience convinced him that others would see the horror of what he had done if he were now belatedly to reveal that he had solicited an original story from Chesterton. He lived in dread that Chesterton would write and ask about it, perhaps in a letter to the president, and his perfidy would be exposed. The thought of the literary giant perusing a magazine from a midwestern campus did not seem preposterous to Horan, but then his conscience gave him no rest.

After graduation, despite a successful academic record to match his athletic prowess, Horan, unlike most alumni, became estranged from his old school. He never returned for games, he did not attend reunions, he was not a contributor. It was as if he were trying to efface years that had been tainted by the Chesterton story. Horan had tried one more time to confess the theft before he graduated, and the priest had told him he was being scrupulous. Leave the story in the *Scholastic* offices and wipe the matter from his mind. But he was given fifteen decades of the rosary for his penance.

Noah conjectured that Horan had never forgiven himself for what he had done and with the passage of years felt increasingly unable to undo his deed. The story hung like an albatross around his neck. He could never forget it. From time to time, he would return to the diary and make an entry and invariably they concerned the event that had cast a pall over his life.

After purchasing them, it took Noah weeks to go through the Horan papers and catalog them. Until he was done he continued to hope against hope that the Chesterton story would be among the things he had bought. It was not. There was only one possibility remaining. The story must have been included in the small cache of papers that had been excluded from the auction and been given to the Notre Dame archives. About to contact the archivist, Noah hesitated. It would not do to alert him that he had such a new treasure in his holdings. After all, there was no certainty that Horan had finally returned the story to its legitimate owner. But there were other thoughts that encouraged Noah's silence, ones he did not articulate fully even to himself. He decided that he must go in person to the archives.

4

versity of Notre Dame was an all-male institution. Saint Mary's, across Highway 31, a woman's college run by sisters of the Congregation of Holy Cross, had its own long and distinguished history. Negotiations had once begun to unite the two institutions, but the nuns had wisely withdrawn from what they saw as a threat of complete absorption and loss of identity. It was then that Notre Dame began to admit women students, not of course in retaliation, but in obedience to the zeitgeist that held that there was something old-fashioned and dubious in an all-male institution. Notre Dame flourished in its new coeducational incarnation and, some thought surprisingly, Saint Mary's took a new lease on life and continued to attract gifted young women. Over the years, Notre Dame's female population approached equality with its male population. This goal had been reached gradually since it entailed the conversion of residence halls to female use as well as the building of new residences.

Amanda Pick had been an undergraduate at Notre Dame. She had lived in Badin Hall, where she had a single room, something she had never had at home. Badin was one of the older residences, just north of a dining hall, near what was then the bookstore. It gave Amanda the sense of being connected with a Notre Dame that would have regarded the presence of women other than nuns on the premises as an anomaly. But she was emphatically of the new breed and felt perfectly at home at Notre Dame. Already in junior year the thought that soon she must graduate and go filled her with sadness. During her senior year she systematically visited every corner of the campus, wanting to impress on her memory the images that she would carry throughout her life. She would go on to graduate school and then . . . But the future stretched vaguely away and she felt no disposition to define it in any detail.

Her major was philosophy.

"None," she had blithely answered when her parents asked her what good such a major was.

"You'll have to work before you marry," her mother said.

"I'm not sure I want to marry."

Her mother smiled. Well, perhaps she was right. Amanda had felt half in love with two boys during her junior year and continued to like them equally in senior year. Jimmy was lean and blond and on the golf team. Richard was her height, hair tousled, and wore a bewildered look. He learned effortlessly and thought he knew nothing. His parents expected him to be a surgeon, but he majored in classics.

Richard got a Rhodes and went to Oxford, while Amanda went off to Saint Andrew's to study with John Haldane. She and Jimmy got together from time to time, but it was as if they had left what linked them back on the campus in South Bend. Jimmy came to play the course, but he was preparing to join the PGA and spend the rest of his life playing golf. For some reason, Amanda found that sad.

"Apply," Professor Haldane urged her, when a tenure track position at Notre Dame appeared in *Jobs in Philosophy*. This was a publication Amanda had begun to read with dread and fascination. Suddenly she was a commodity, someone with an area of concentration as well as areas of competency. When she sent off her CV to Notre Dame she had the feeling that someone else was doing it. What if they were interested in her? Did she really want to return to South Bend?

They were interested, the job was offered, and she accepted. Her parents were ecstatic. They seemed to think that she had worked out a plan and then put it gradually into

26

action. Her father all but apologized for thinking her impractical.

"I suppose you'll marry another philosopher," her mother said.

"I'm not sure I want to marry."

And of course her mother smiled. But she could not see herself married to either Richard or Jimmy. Jimmy was a nomad now, traveling from tournament to tournament and showing up on television now and again. Richard had taken a job with an experimental college in California, where he taught Latin and Greek. Everyone was a tutor, there were no ranks, the pay was terrible, Richard loved it. It occurred to Amanda that Richard's life was like that of a monk. Maybe he did have a religious vocation.

"Only if I could say mass in Latin."

"Isn't that allowed?"

"Tolerated."

He did say the office every day, in Latin. Amanda lit candles for him and for Jimmy at the grotto, but she might have been commemorating the past. Meanwhile she had to think about getting tenure.

"The decision will be made after six years," Horst, the chair, explained to her. "You will be expected to publish and become active in the profession."

She had to do well as a teacher too, but that seemed less important. It was the custom to grant a half year's leave during the six probationary years so that one could more easily meet the scholarly requirements for tenure.

Amanda read a paper on Frege at the eastern meeting of the APA. Two notes on logical matters were accepted for publication, one in *Mind* the other in *Vivarium*. But then, prompted by memories of Professor Pottery's course, which she had taken as an undergraduate, she reread *Orthodoxy* and *The Everlasting Man* and became enamored of Chesterton. Of course she kept this a secret. After she recommended *Orthodoxy* to a student, Bridget Quirk stopped by to see her.

27

"What's this about orthodoxy?"

"You mean the book."

"Is it a book?"

"What did you think it was?"

"It sounded rather . . ."

"I suppose it did."

"A book, you say?"

"By an Englishman named Chesterton."

"Chesterton."

Perhaps she was thinking of the town to the west of South Bend. Amanda diverted Bridget by giving her an offprint of her Frege paper. The visit had been warning enough. It would not do to go against the prevailing orthodoxy as to what constituted philosophy and what did not.

Glimpses of Sean Pottery brought home to Amanda the range that had characterized her undergraduate years at Notre Dame. Both Latin and French, history in quantity, and literature, although no class had impressed her as much as Sean Pottery's had. He was an intimidating model of what a teacher should be. Had she chosen philosophy rather than English so that she could adapt the ideal rather than merely imitate it? Graduate work had been a necessary means of getting into the classroom. Roger Knight, bless him, understood her attitude toward the criteria for tenure.

"Do you know what Benjamin Jowett said about research?"

She had to ask who Jowett was, but she shared the great man's attitude toward the Teutonic ideal of scholarship. Giving *The Coloured Lands* to Sean Pottery had been impulsive. She might as easily have given it to Roger Knight. In any case, the event began her almost clandestine affair with Gilbert Keith Chesterton. In her study at home she had a blowup of a photograph of the writer. He was disheveled and fat and wore a cape and a slouch hat. The first time she saw Roger Knight she had the crazy notion that he was Chesterton redivivus.

"Did anyone ever tell you you look like Chesterton?"

28

"The town?" His laughter strengthened the allusion.

"The writer."

"Father Brown."

"You know him?"

He found the question surprising. "Everyone knows Chesterton."

"I don't," his brother, Philip, said. "I used to smoke Chesterfields though."

The thing about Roger Knight was that she could discuss her technical papers with him as well as her passion for Chesterton. He seemed to have read everything and had the knack unknown to her own generation of being able to recite the poetry he loved from memory. He had Chesterton's "Lepanto" at his command and on one memorable occasion had recited the whole poem, acting it out, while Amanda and Philip sat enthralled, the sole audience for this virtuoso performance. Amanda entertained the velleity that she herself would memorize some of the shorter poems. But why? Memory was a capacity of computers. Any page could be photocopied at will.

"There is a Chesterton web site," she said to Roger.

"I believe there are several."

Meaning there were. He lacked the academic need to trump any conversational card played. And, of course, he had been spared the ordeal of coming up for tenure.

But she had not told even Roger Knight about the event that had brought to an abrupt end her friendship with Sean Pottery.

Pottery was older than her father and she had never in a million years thought there was any danger of anything other than friendship, if listening to him hold forth could be the basis of friendship. But they got along. She had stopped thinking of him as a senior member of the faculty, and, she realized later, he had stopped making references to himself as the twentieth-century equivalent of Methuselah. And then one night at ten o'clock he arrived at her door in a cab. Her first thought was that Laura, with whom she shared the house, had cut short her visit to Chicago. The cab was disappearing up the street when she opened the door. Surprised though she was, she did not hesitate to ask Pottery in. His entrance was unsteady, but once he was seated in a chair he seemed all right. He was never completely sober at this time of night, of course, but she had not thought it imprudent to offer him another scotch and water. When he showed her his empty glass ten minutes later, she hesitated, then took it into the kitchen. To her surprise, he followed her. When she turned toward him, there was an expression in his eyes she had never seen before. It was beseeching, it was tragic, it was melting. His breath came in gasps. Suddenly he lunged at her and tried to take her in his arms. She pirouetted free, and this caused him to lose his balance. He fell. The sound of his head hitting the floor seemed to echo in the room as he lay there motionless.

During the next few minutes, Amanda aged. She was certain she had a dead man lying on her kitchen floor. Explanations rattled through her mind, all of them unconvincing. Yet how could she possibly tell what had actually happened? And then he groaned.

She got him into a seated position and handed him the drink she had prepared. It seemed to restore him. She helped him to his feet and into the living room. Neither of them mentioned what had happened in the kitchen. Amanda wondered if he even remembered.

The next time he came to the house he was already so far gone in drink that Amanda did not open the door to him, but neither did she entirely shut him out. Through the outer storm door he loudly declared his love for her, studding his slurred effusion with snatches of poetry appropriate to the occasion. From time to time he would interrupt himself and pound upon the door.

"Who in the world is it?" Laura asked, emerging sleepily from her room.

"It's all right."

"It's Professor Pottery! What is he shouting?"

"Poetry."

"What time is it?"

Gradually it dawned on Laura that there was a drunken professor on their doorstep at one in the morning speaking in loud tones. "He means you," Laura said. Pottery had pressed his face against the glass and formed with elaborate but silent elocution the words *I love you*.

"He's drunk."

"Amanda, he'll wake the neighborhood. If you can't call the police, someone else will."

The remark was prophetic. Five minutes later the light from a patrol car began to play across the lawn, and then Professor Pottery was caught in its beam. He swept off his beret and bowed to the light. The dipping motion ruined his balance, and he tumbled over into a bush. Two policeman came running up the walk.

"Does he live here?" one of the officers asked.

Laura said, "He is a professor and he has been sexually harassing us."

"Laura!"

"Did you receive a call of complaint?" Laura demanded of the officer.

But the policeman was disinclined to bring Laura up to speed on his duties. A minute later the patrol car pulled away with Pottery in the backseat. It might have been imagination, but Amanda thought she could hear him reciting Poe's "To Helen."

Whatever the police did with Professor Pottery that night was their secret. There was no news item of a drunken professor being arrested in the middle of the night reciting love poetry to a junior colleague at the top of his lungs.

"They wouldn't arrest a professor, Laura."

"You're probably right. And they were men. Men protect one another. You're lucky they didn't arrest you for enticing aged faculty to your doorstep."

The following day Laura began her campaign. Amanda must report Pottery's unwanted advances. She owed it to herself and to every other woman in the academic world.

"Laura, he's just a tipsy old man."

Laura was bitter, of course, and not without reason.

The next time Professor Pottery visited it was a Sunday afternoon, but it was still Saturday night for him. He had been drinking nonstop for hours. Amanda let him in, considering that the lesser of two evils. Laura had gone off for brunch with a number of friends who shared her attitude toward males. To Amanda's great relief, Pottery fell immediately asleep in the chair she put him in. He looked like a great ruddy-faced baby sleeping there. He slept for two hours. When Laura's car pulled into the driveway, Amanda began to shake him awake. He came confusedly into consciousness, he looked at her, puzzled, and then a beatific expression spread over his face and he rose to his feet.

"Amanda," he cried, "my darling gerundive; she who must be loved."

He lurched toward her and she caught him in her arms. Understandably perhaps, when Laura came into the room she assumed that Amanda was being attacked. She slid her purse from her shoulder, got a grip on the strap, and then like David unleashing on Goliath, swung the purse in a great arc and caught Pottery behind the ear. She repeated this before Amanda, who had broken free of the amorous professor, could stop her. But the second blow with the purse felled him, and he sprawled upon the floor.

"How did he get in?"

"Laura, I let him in."

Laura ignored the prone professor and looked sadly at Amanda. "Oh, this is classical"

The meaning of this would be brought home to Amanda again and again over the next weeks. But at the moment it was necessary to take care of Pottery. Laura wanted to call the police, but Amanda countered with the suggestion that she call Roger Knight.

"You see, you're protecting him, too."

Maybe she was. Roger and his brother, Philip, arrived in a van and took in the situation immediately. All Amanda told them on that occasion was that the professor had apparently drunk too much and had collapsed. Philip cradled the conked-out Pottery in his arms and carried him out to the van.

It was difficult to know how much of these events stayed in Pottery's mind when relative sobriety returned. But the uncontrolled love he professed to feel for Amanda when he was drunk was replaced by a chilly hostility when sober. He resented her reaction to his advances, particularly calling in the Knight brothers. Her efforts to get them back onto a neutral plane failed. He was particularly resistant to the topic of Chesterton. Meanwhile Laura explained to Amanda that she was exhibiting the classical reaction to sexual harassment.

"Sexual harassment? He tried to kiss me."

"He forced himself on you."

The trouble with Laura's descriptions was that, however true, they did not seem to be the whole truth. Amanda tried to discuss the problem with Roger, certain he would see it differently than Laura; but the massive and sympathetic Roger seemed to have difficulty understanding what she was saying. Finally Amanda gave up, feeling she was corrupting youth to bother Roger with this story. But Philip Knight came to her office, and it was clear he understood what was happening. "We sobered him up but before we did he went on and on about you."

"He's harmless, of course. My roommate doesn't think so, however."

Philip shrugged. "I hope you're right and she's wrong."

5

Inn within view of the campus and walked to the library in order to work in the archives. He had made an appointment with Father Finn, but it was still not firm when he spoke with Wendy, the chief archivist, and told her of his Chesterton holdings.

"I feel guilty owning all those things. They should be available to everyone."

"But aren't you a dealer?"

"Selling them would just relocate the problem." He looked beyond the office at her domain. "They should be here."

"Do you have a list of the items?" Her tone altered. "And the asking price?"

"Oh, I would donate them."

"Have you met Father Finn?" she cried.

"I called his office and tried to make an appointment."

"Tried?"

She picked up the phone and dialed a number. Minutes later, after a brisk exchange, a luncheon had been arranged for the following day at the Morris Inn. "I will make certain that he understands the significance of your holdings."

"I thought you just did that."

"That was for starters." On the phone, Wendy had made it unequivocally clear that a donation of massive importance to the archives was quivering on the horizon and that all stops should be pulled to smooth the way to the benefaction. Listening to her, Noah had felt a bit like a sacrificial lamb being readied for the slaughter. Is this how the wealthy feel when they visit their alma mater? Donations of money were essential to the flourishing of an institution like Notre Dame, but the money was needed, after buildings and maintenance and salaries and all the rest, for the purchase of such items as Noah's Chesterton collection. He gave Wendy a copy of the items he was prepared to part with, not everything he had, of course, but enough to stir the collective cupidity of the staff of the archives.

"Could I see what you already have of Chesterton?"

Thus he had been introduced to Greg Whelan. The assistant archivist got him settled at a computer and gave him a few clues as to how to conduct his search and then went away. Fifteen minutes later, he pulled a chair up next to Noah's. He was holding the sheet Noah had given Wendy. He was trying to speak. Obviously he was impressed. Noah, in turn, was impressed by the university's Chesterton holdings, most of them the gift of a Tulsa alumnus named Shaw, who was still a legend among book dealers. Not every collector has an oil field to underwrite his purchases.

"You have the holograph of the Notre Dame poem, "The Arena'?"

"Would you like to see it?"

"May I?"

Noah was persona grata in the archives, no doubt of that. From time to time he felt a twinge of pain at the price he was going to pay for gaining such easy entrée, but his objective was worth it. His donation was meant to allay any misgivings about having a rare book dealer on the premises. During the first day he established his knowledgability with Whelan and became friendly with the stammering archivist. It was amazing to find a man with Whelan's knowledge and training spending his life performing the menial tasks of an archivist. On the other hand, where else could he have at his fingertips such treasures? Whelan's grasp of the history of Notre Dame lore was vast. The first day Noah went off to lunch with Whelan at the Huddle, where

36

in the chaotic noise and bustle Whelan forgot to stutter and proved to be a delightful companion. It was clear to Noah that Whelan was going to be his open sesame. But he would have to be careful: the Renaissance sweep of Whelan's knowledge might make him suspicious when he learned of Noah's interest in the *Scholastic*. But he laid the groundwork early.

"Horan was on the staff of the *Scholastic*."

"He left a few things to us."

"Are they in the database?"

"They're not catalogued yet." Whelan sighed. "We're far from adequately staffed, and of course we are running out of space."

Noah encouraged the lamentation. The leitmotif was that the Horan materials had thus far received only a preliminary treatment.

"Maybe I could help."

"They're in storage."

Noah did not press it but later that afternoon he learned that the archives was granted extra space in the basement of Holy Cross House. That is where the Horan papers must be and, with them, what he had come for—the holograph copy of a hitherto unknown Chesterton Father Brown story, a manuscript whose existence had eaten at Horan's conscience during his long life.

6

lens of her own unfortunate experience, was convinced that Amanda was in mortal danger from the aroused professor of English.

"Laura, take a good look at him. He's an old man."

"Old or young, they're still men."

Amanda might have laughed it off. The only time she had felt unease with a man was when a stranger sat down abruptly at her table in the Huddle and said, "You're Amanda Pick."

He was too old to be a student, and if he was on the faculty she had never seen him before. "That's right."

"You share a house with Laura Flynn."

"What is it you want?"

"Laura and I were married. At least I thought we were."

"You're Tony?" This man was a far cry from the monster Laura had described. "Have you come to see her?" There leapt up in Amanda's mind that all Laura's grievances could be swept away if only she were reunited with the man she insisted had been her husband; she didn't care what any marriage court said. But Tony laughed bitterly. "She won't see me."

"Have you been to the house?"

"She looked out and as soon as she saw who it was she slammed the door in my face."

Amanda did not know what to say. It was too easy to imagine Laura closing the door on her former husband, if that is what he was. She asked him what had happened between him and Laura.

"I'm sure she has given you an earful on that subject."

"She said you got an annulment."

"Is that what she told you?"

"What did happen?"

If Tony could be believed, there hadn't been a divorce let alone an annulment. Nor had he objected to Laura's academic career. "I would have preferred her staying home, sure, but I didn't try to stop her. That wasn't the problem. Her consciousness was raised." He said the last sentence with deep sarcasm. He meant that Laura had become a feminist.

"There wasn't an annulment?"

"How could there be? We are as married as anyone."

The more she heard, the more confused Amanda became. But the occasion seemed a rare opportunity to help Laura and Tony out of the impasse their lives had reached. In the end she offered to intercede with Laura.

"Where can I reach you?" she asked Tony Ryan.

"I have a room at the Ramada Inn."

Amanda went immediately home, certain that Laura would not have left the house after closing the door on Tony. Without fanfare, she went directly to the point. Laura nodded when Amanda asked if her husband had come to the house.

"He looked you up, didn't he? I should have called your office and warned you."

"Laura, what really did happen between the two of you?"

Laura stared at her. A full minute went by before she spoke. "What did he tell you?"

Laura sank into a chair during Amanda's recital of the exchange in the Huddle. A kaleidoscope of expressions raced across her face, but through them all the tears poured from her eyes. "Those are all lies, Amanda. Everything he said was a lie."

"He said there was no divorce, no annulment."

Laura sprang to her feet and ran into her room. There was the sound of the closet door, something hit the floor. In a

40

moment Laura was back, waving a sheet of paper. "Tell me what that is!"

Amanda took it. The letterhead was of the diocesan marriage court of Rochester. A Monsignor Boyle informed Laura that her marriage to Anthony Ryan had been annulled by the court on which he served. There was a provision for appeal, if she cared to pursue one. Amanda looked up at Laura, who was now weeping uncontrollably. She stood and took her in her arms, utterly confused.

Laura was not, accordingly, a sympathetic listener when Amanda spoke ruefully of Sean Pottery. Amanda tried to blame Pottery, but how could she fail to see that if only she had reacted differently, things might have been otherwise? For all she knew, she might have been encouraging him; of course she had been. Every woman flirts at least mildly with any man; the thing with Pottery was that there had seemed no danger that either of them would have seen that kind of sequel to their friendship. And now it had ended. Where once there had been a friend, now there was an enemy. Only when he drank did he remember how he truly felt about her. Sober, he could push such thoughts from his mind. No doubt Amanda reminded him of what may have been a solitary lapse from his Olympian indifference to the female sex. It hurt to be treated like a semi-stranger after their lively conversations. Chesterton had been a link between them; now he was like a wall. She sensed that Pottery resented her interest in his great liter⸍ Sometimes she almost wished that she had not rea⸍ d that night in her kitchen. Sean Pottery no l⸍ sibly old to her. She found that, in re⸍ by his interest. Sometimes she fa⸍ have happened. They might have⸍

Laura shook her head. "M⸍ solution."

Amanda ended by acc⸍ happened to her marriag⸍

her desire for an academic career. They had broken up by mutual agreement, a kind of furlough from their marriage; but one day Laura received a letter informing her that he had obtained an annulment, the letter that Amanda had seen. This meant that their marriage had never existed. Why had Tony lied to Amanda about what he had done? It was the metaphysical aspects of the thing that caused anguish to Laura. "How can something that happened never have happened?"

"Not even God can accomplish that."

"Oh? Well, his representatives think they can. You saw the letter."

Of course the letter from the diocesan marriage court meant that the past had not been what Laura thought it was, not that it no longer was what it had been. But Laura was not interested in analytical niceties. For all that, she was a pleasant housemate, as long as the conversation did not turn to marriage.

FATHER FINN HAD INVITED FATHER
Carmody and Roger Knight to the lunch he was giving for
Noah, the priest one of the legendary figures on campus and
Knight a proud new acquisition, occupant of the Huneker Chair
for Catholic Studies. Everyone but Roger was astonished that
the name of Huneker should be familiar to Noah; Roger would
only have been surprised if Noah had not known Huneker.

"Professor Pottery should be here, too," Father Carmody
said. "He's our resident Chesterton expert."

"I asked him," Finn protested. "You know how he is."

"He's in love," Roger said brightly.

"In love!" The two priests stared at the massive Huneker
Professor.

"Infatuated may be a better word. If he were not the age he
is, I would call it puppy love."

"Puppy love!"

This was not the conversational gambit Father Finn would
have chosen; but once Roger got them started, they stayed with
it, and after all, Pottery was connected with the point of the
luncheon, Noah's expressed desire, if only to the archivist, to
make a gift of some priceless papers related to the immortal
Chesterton. Noah himself perked up when he heard the name of
the object of Pottery's affections. Amanda had arrived at the
archives just as he was leaving for this luncheon date, and Greg
Whelan had introduced them. Noah had not expected to find
such a lovely creature in the archives, and then to be told that
she was a professor of philosophy as well . . .

"Assistant professor," she had corrected Whelan's introduction.

"I am still impressed."

Whelan whispered that she was up for tenure this year and understandably on edge about it. Noah had found her serene and, if not beautiful, extremely attractive. She reminded him of a woman he had met at the Milan Book Fair several years before. Within hours they had been close, everything quite moral and adult, but what he'd felt was unlike what he had ever felt before. But the fair ended and she went back to her store in Bari, and he returned to Saint Louis. A few E-mails and faxes had been inadequate to sustain the magic. She had her career; he had his. The memory had faded, but it was stirred again when he met Amanda Pick and he could believe that his susceptibility to Victoria had been merely fanfare for this. But going down in the elevator to be picked up in the circle by Father Finn and Roger Knight, Noah had decompressed. He had come to Notre Dame for a very specific purpose and must not be deflected from it.

Roger Knight was someone Noah already knew by name. The little book on Baron Corvo had found its way into the second-hand market and was a much sought after item. This was somewhat surprising, given its popularity and sales.

"Apparently those who own it don't want to get rid of it."

"Maybe I should urge the publisher to reissue it."

"Please don't. No, I don't mean that. The value of the first edition wouldn't be affected by that."

Roger seemed to be entirely without ego, a surprise in an author. He launched immediately into a discussion of Chesterton. "You couldn't find a better place for any papers of his," he assured Noah.

"I came by most of what I have when I bought the papers of a graduate of Notre Dame named Horan."

"What year?" Father Carmody asked. "There have been many Horans who've graduated from Notre Dame."

44

"1931."

"Henry Horan?"

"Did you know him?

"Of course I knew him. He was on the football team when I was a freshman."

"Halfback."

"An outstanding student as well as player. But after he graduated, he just drifted away. . . . "

"You would never know that from his papers."

"The things he gave the archives are valuable," Roger said, but his tone seemed to suggest that they were not as valuable as they might have been.

"I was told they haven't been catalogued yet."

"Whelan let me look through them."

Noah held his breath. Surely if Roger had come upon the Father Brown story he would have noticed it. Everything Noah had learned of it assured him that it was written in the author's own very distinctive handwriting. But Roger said nothing further.

"The things Horan held back are very interesting. I left the list with the archivist."

"Greg Whelan showed it to me. I wonder why he held them back."

"You've definitely decided to give the Henry Horan papers to the university?"

"That's really why I'm here, Father." Noah winced inwardly to have his gift identified simply as "the Horan papers," but of course that's what they were.

"I wish he himself had made the gift," Father Carmody said.

Was it only imagination that made Noah think that the old priest suspected why Henry Horan had been reluctant to do that?

The lunch at the Morris Inn was what Noah had expected, being shmoozed by Father Finn. In the course of the meal, Finn conducted him to the corner table where the president sat with his guests, several Italian prelates. Finn conveyed the purpose of Noah's visit.

"Stop by and see me while you're here."

"Thank you, Father. I'll do that."

When Finn related the invitation after they returned to their own table, Father Carmody said, "You should stop in and say hello to Father Ted, too. He and Ned Joyce have offices in the library."

"Just drop in?"

"Mention Chesterton," Finn said.

"And Henry Horan," Carmody added.

"So you teach philosophy?" Noah said to Amanda Pick the following day. Throughout the morning, he had surreptitiously watched her work, and when finally she took a break and stepped outside the archives, he'd sauntered out to say hello.

"You sound surprised."

"I didn't mean to."

"I thought maybe you noticed what I was working on."

"Whelan told me."

"Told you what?"

Words seemed to be means of touching her, of eliciting one expression after another, all of them fascinating. Her intelligence seemed the reason for her physical attractiveness, soul to its body, and her face was a remarkable theater of thoughts made visible.

"He mentioned that you had an interest in Chesterton."

She smiled. "And he mentioned to me that you were going to donate some Chesterton papers to the archives."

"I wonder if all benefactors lose their anonymity so quickly."

But of course it was only a tight little circle who knew of his benefaction and would be affected by it. Pottery had come blustering importantly into the archives the second day Noah was on campus and scanned the list of the Henry Horan papers with raised, supercilious brows. "The duplicates aside," he said,

46

seeming to speak through his nostrils, "there are one or two interesting things here."

"What would you single out, Professor?" Noah asked with feigned deference. What a pompous ass.

Pottery looked wearily at the list again. "The exchange of letters with Eric Gill could be interesting."

At least he had seized upon the most valuable item in the papers Noah was giving. Pottery's frown deepened as he continued to study the list.

"Who is this?"

"Huneker. James Huneker."

"But who is he?"

"Ask Roger Knight. His endowed chair is named for Huneker."

A bloodshot eye bore into Noah at this suggestion that Pottery might seek knowledge from anyone else, let alone the Huneker Chair of Catholic Studies. Whatever interest Pottery had in the Horan papers fled. He left the archives without even asking to see the Gill/Chesterton correspondence.

Noah mentioned the Pottery episode to Amanda when they had gone outside so she could have a cigarette. Noah waved away her offer.

"Nobody smokes anymore," she lamented.

"I smoke a pipe. And an occasional cigar."

"So light your pipe."

He shook his head. "I don't like a hurried smoke. I can wait."

"Until when?"

"Until after we've had dinner."

She tried not to smile. "And when will that be?"

"I hope tonight."

"How long will you be staying?"

"That depends."

But she mastered the impulse to ask what it depended on, sensing that it was a kind of trap. So he added, "Days, a week. I find the archives fascinating."

What would this principled, intelligent woman think if she knew that the purpose of his visit was to take possession of the Father Brown story over which Henry Horan had agonized throughout his long life and, in the end, included without fanfare in an otherwise modest bequest to his alma mater? It was bad enough to come as a thief, but it was worse to disguise himself as a benefactor of the university to conceal his real purpose. The important thing was to take possession of the story before anyone discovered it was in the archives.

"I met Roger Knight," he said to Amanda.

"Isn't he wonderful?" The real question was whether the huge professor had made a careful examination of the papers Henry Horan had given. But no one who'd come upon that story could possibly have kept quiet about it. That being so, Whelan could not have found it either.

That night he and Amanda went to the Vezuvio where the pasta was adequate when taken with lots of red wine. To Noah's surprise Barolo was available. It was a vintage Amanda had never had, so he had the added pleasure of introducing her to what is arguably the best Italian red of all.

"Tell me about Amanda."

"Do you want a quick course in philosophy?"

"Someone said you're up for tenure this year."

Her face clouded and he realized he had tapped into her deepest present concern. He asked her to explain it to him, and she outlined the process whereby a teacher moved into the ranks of the tenured faculty. It was pretty clear that a negative decision on tenure was all but the kiss of death to an academic career.

"Imagine applying for a job when it is clear to everyone that you were not judged worth keeping by another department. Who wants to second guess them or seem to be taking other schools' rejects?"

"You must have published."

The book on Frege sounded impressive as did the half-dozen articles she had published in prestigious journals, but she did not recount these achievements with pride or confidence.

"The problem is, what have I done for them lately. It's been three years since my last philosophical article was published, and what I have written just won't count. Oh, it's my fault. It became clear to me that students had to be led gradually into philosophy, and I began to use works by C. S. Lewis and Chesterton. Then I go on to Josef Pieper and finally look at some primary texts."

"That sounds sensible."

"It is sensible. And it is important to show that philosophy is not just a game that professionals play for their own amusement. But this goes against the drive toward more specialization and professionalization. The very emphasis on 'research' is a sign of that. Why not judge a teacher primarily as a teacher."

She stopped and shook her head impatiently. "You don't want to hear all this."

"Whelan said you had written some things on Chesterton."

"They're among the things that don't count."

"Hasn't Professor Pottery made a career out of his interest in Chesterton?"

"Oh, he's in English."

"He's also proof that interest in an interesting author doesn't make one interesting."

"You've met him."

"He blew into the archives yesterday and condescended to me."

"He is really very shy."

"And Atilla the Hun was timid."

She laughed. He poured her another glass of Barolo. They got along. He wanted to ask her if she would drop out of the academic life if she were refused tenure, but stating the negative possibility would doubtless have depressed her. At her door, he shook her hand, just friends, and went back to the Jamison.

8

ton did not diminish after the unfortunate contretemps with
Professor Pottery in her kitchen. What would she have done if
she had not had Roger to talk with about her work on Chesterton's visit to Notre Dame? In Roger's eyes, Amanda was the
expert in the matter of Chesterton, and he usually deferred to
her. When she worked in the archives, Amanda found herself
pursuing her avocation to the exclusion of philosophical
research, following the spoor of curiosity through the papers of
the archives. It was almost as if she had been in search of what
she eventually found. She was so excited she just had to speak
of it, and thank God there was Roger.

"A hitherto unknown Father Brown story! Is it possible?"

"Shhh. Isn't it incredible?"

"Tell me about it."

"Apparently he wrote it while he was here," she said,
squeezing his arm.

"Of course there is the famous poem about Notre Dame
football."

His eyes went out of focus and for a moment she thought he
was going to recite it, but of course it was Pottery who would
have done that. Roger's mind was on the news of her extraordinary discovery. "I wish you had told me this while we were still
in the archives. I'm dying to see it."

She had hurried him off to the Huddle—to the degree that
hurry was possible for Roger—and they sat at a table out of the

flow, lost in the sea of students. Amanda, having looked around, opened her briefcase and let him peek.

"They let you take it out of the archives?"

"You mustn't tell."

He waved his hand. "Rules are made to be broken."

He seemed to think that she had removed the treasure with permission. She did not correct the impression. And then his face lit up. "This will assure your getting tenure."

What a dear man! She put her hand on his. Did he really think the philosophy department's appointment and tenure committee would regard the discovery of a lost work of Chesterton's sufficient basis for a favorable tenure decision? They were expecting more things like her monograph on Frege as her ticket into permanent status on the faculty. Moreover, there was only one permanent slot, her rival for which was Hans Wiener, known with ambiguous affection as "Hot Dog" by the students.

9

whimpering child cradled in his arms, Hans Wiener paced the upstairs hallway of his rented home, giving Teresa respite from the colicky Conor and hoping the twins would sleep through this nocturnal disturbance. Hans had changed the baby and unsuccessfully tempted it with a bottle, but Conor was not yet weaned and wanted the breast of the exhausted Teresa. How many harried fathers had considered letting their whimpering young nuzzle at their chests, finding at least a pacifier in the biologically useless male nipple? Even at Notre Dame he and Teresa had to explain the number of their offspring.

"Is your wife Catholic?"

"And fecund."

He and Teresa were Catholics of the strict observance, but it was not church policy that explained the three children and, though this was still their secret, a fourth on the way—so much for the theory that prolonged breast feeding naturally forestalled conception. With Hans and Teresa, it was a question of love, an absence of calculation, to some extent an ecological matter, not wishing to fool with Mother Nature. What joy could compare with that of tumbling about in their king-size bed with their squealing young?

Bridget Quirk had undertaken to speak to Teresa about it.

"She seemed to think that we thought having lots of children would put pressure on the department in your tenure decision."

"Did she say that?"

"Not in so many words. She's an analytic philosopher. She speaks with forked tongue."

Hans was furious. Was Bridget accusing him of trying to breed his way to advancement? She herself was a lapsed Catholic.

"I mean I lapse into it from time to time. I make my Easter duty."

She spoke like that. She remembered the church prior to Vatican II and was wont to recall it in hushed and horrified tones. She remembered 1968 and the uproar over Paul VI's *Humanae Vitae*.

"What does that mean?"

" 'Human life.' It's the encyclical in which he tried to reestablish the old ban on birth control."

Bridget was a grass widow whose husband had gone off to the supermarket one day and never came back, or so at least the story went. Her notion of religion seemed to be sexual liberation, though as far as Hans could see she lived like a nun, a preconciliar nun. Her notion of the Second Vatican Council was that it opened the windows to the sexual revolution: Haight Asbury, Woodstock, pot. Bridget had led the campaign for a smoke-free campus and was also ethical consultant to a national group that sought to legalize marijuana. She taught virtue ethics and was a foe of moral absolutes.

"I expect to be judged on the basis of my publications," Hans told Bridget. "They are more than enough to warrant a favorable judgment."

It was stupid to confront Bridget with what she had said to Teresa, but he was damned if he would let her insinuation go unchallenged.

"Then you have nothing to worry about."

That reply stayed in his mind afterward, enigmatic, sibylline. He found he could not repeat it to Teresa. Spoken without intonation, her expression uninformative, it had the sound of a threat.

It was cruel that he and Amanda Pick were locked in mortal combat for the single permanent slot. They had been hired at the same time so both came up for tenure together. Only one of them could get it. In his heart of hearts, Hans did think that his wife and children should count toward a favorable decision, not exclusively of course, but as tie breakers if the committee judged Amanda and himself equally worthy on a purely academic basis. Also in his heart of hearts, Hans considered himself a far better philosopher than Amanda.

"If only she weren't a woman," Teresa lamented.

Affirmative action still stalked the academic world, giving special consideration to women and minorities and, in the case of Notre Dame, members of the Congregation of the Holy Cross, the religious order that had founded the university in the person of Edward Sorin in 1842. Hans was a liberal politically, but he did not think it fair that Amanda's gender should weigh in the balance against him. Why not then take into account his wife and all the hungry mouths he must fill?

"She wastes her time on nonphilosophical research." Hans did not like to feed Teresa's resentment, but facts were facts.

"What is her teaching like?"

Amanda was scandalously popular in the classroom, so much so that a question had been raised as to the quality of her courses. Could serious philosophy produce such an enthusiastic response? It emerged that she worked with a very expansive notion of philosophy, at least so far as undergraduate teaching was concerned.

"We must first engage their minds," she had said.

"And then marry them?" asked Moutard, bald, exophthalmic, into denial so far as retirement went. " 'Let me not to the marriage of true minds admit impediments.' "

" 'Love is not love that alters when it alteration finds.' " Amanda had continued the quote, and silence had fallen over the meeting.

Maybe Lucretius had done philosophy in verse, but centuries had passed since then, and prose was in the driver's seat. It was one thing for Moutard to wax poetic, but for an untenured assistant professor to choose rhyme over reason was perilous.

If Hans was encouraged by the doubts that some entertained about the range of Amanda's interests, particularly by the raised eyebrows of Horace Cheval and the wet, disapproving noise made by Bridget Quirk, these two arbiters of tenure gave him little confidence in his own prospects.

"Of course she's for Amanda," Teresa said, with narrowed eyes.

"Don't be so sure."

"Did you give them offprints of your recent article?"

He had published a three-page note on a short paragraph in *Beyond Good and Evil*. The journal's referees had praised it to the skies; the editor of *Isis* introduced it with a laudatory note.

Cheval had accepted the offprint with starchy formality, his eyes had scanned the title, he'd given no indication of his initial reaction. "Ah, Nietzsche," Bridget Quirk had said, laying the offprint on her desk after glancing at what he had given her. That night he tried to recapture the tone of the remark for Teresa.

"It sounds to me like she was impressed."

Hans wished that it had sounded that way to him at the time. But like Cheval, Bridget Quirk was impossible to read.

10

THOSE WHO LIVE THEIR LIVES IN
the workaday world are wont to think of the academic life as
almost angelic in its absence of the slings and arrows that
define their own grimmer existence. Indifference to this world's
goods, selflessly transmitting to the young treasures gained
during years of reading and meditating, rejoicing in one's colleagues' good fortune, self-effacing and humble—such are the
otherworldly traits of the academic as envisaged by the envious
citizen of the quotidian world. There were of course some professors who approached this altruistic ideal. Others not so
much fell short of it as wholly ignored this inhuman standard.
By and large, however, or so thought Roger Knight, university
faculty were among the nicest of people. There were days when
his heart all but burst with joy at his good fortune to have been
named the Huneker professor of Catholic Studies.

"Huneker?" he had queried, when Father Carmody came
on a visit to Rye with the intention of discovering if Roger
might be interested in being named the first occupant of the
endowed chair.

"There is no reason why you should know who Huneker
was."

"But I do know." Roger gave his wheeled work chair a push
and glided backward toward a bookshelf from which he
removed a fat, green volume. Kunitz & Haycraft, twentieth-
century authors, a volume into which Huneker had just made it.
"I didn't know he had a connection with Notre Dame, however."

"He didn't. The donor is a Philadelphian whose wife is a

grandniece of the great man. The chair will establish, not com-memorate, a connection between Huneker and Notre Dame."

"What a splendid idea."

"I doubt that there are many who recognize his name."

"Other than grandnieces?"

Roger had still not guessed that Father Carmody was sounding him out for the proposed endowed chair. They spoke of Roger's book on Frederick Rolfe, aka Baron Corvo, an eccentric Scot who had attracted the attention of many. Roger's book had taken Corvo's Catholicism seriously.

Roger had received his doctorate from Princeton at the age of nineteen, a prodigy who was a puzzle to himself and to most others. His age and his ballooning weight had made an aca-demic career unfeasible, and after a stint in the navy during which he had heroically, if only temporarily, rid himself of excess weight, he and his brother, Phil, had settled in Rye, from which redoubt Phil conducted his private investigator business, running an ad in the yellow pages of various cities around the nation, giving only an eight hundred number, as well as having a web page on the Internet. He selected clients with care. Roger had become, in effect, his assistant, obtaining in the process his own private investigator's license. It was that rather than his Ph.D. that had seemed his passport to the real world. Not that he had ever turned from the life of the mind. His correspondence, largely E-mail, was voluminous, his inter-ests vast and unpredictable, his reputation among a dozen world-class scholars of the highest. He had even lured the Luddite and therefore reluctant Alasdair MacIntyre into an E-mail correspondence. None of this was known to Father Car-mody when he came to Rye. He had discerned in the Corvo book a disposition to pursue the Catholic spoor down the nights and down the days and down the labyrinthine ways of Western culture.

"Francis Thompson," Roger said.

"I am not testing you," Father Carmody said.

"But I love being tested."

The chair was offered, and after consultation with Philip, Roger accepted. The Knight brothers moved to South Bend, where a cornucopia of athletic seasons and constant intellectual stimulus gladdened the hearts of both. The proximity of senior professors of note was a joy, but Roger took equal delight in the company of junior faculty still on the lower rungs of the academic ascent, young people like Amanda Pick and Hans Wiener.

Roger found it cruel that two such promising young people must vie for a single permanent spot in their department. They were as unlike as members of the same profession could possibly be, good in quite different ways. Hans was an expert in the various versions of postmodernism that emanated from Europe, largely from a Paris heavily influenced by German philosophy. His papers were impenetrable and exegetic and highly regarded by his peers. Of course the majority of the department members thought the authors he studied were demented and their positions incoherent.

"That is the point!"

"Not having a point?"

Hans would sigh. It was so difficult to communicate to the hermeneutically handicapped.

Amanda, influenced by Peter Geach, had become interested in Frege and gone on to the thought of Elizabeth Anscombe and Iris Murdoch, mastering these to a degree that lent a slightly ventriloquial air to her work. Murdoch perhaps had provided a kind of warrant for wandering from the philosophical reservation into the more pleasant fields of belles lettres.

"Once there were men of letters," she complained to Roger. "Now there are only experts."

It was a view they shared and Roger delighted her with his praise of Aldous Huxley's essay on Maine de Baran, a feat of which few professional philosophers were now capable, and of course there were no more Huxleys in the world.

"*The Devils of Loudon,*" Amanda added, albeit with hesitation.

Roger had a theory about Huxley's interest in this convent riven by diabolical possession and a perverse chaplain. It was on a line that led inexorably to Huxley's praise of peyote in *The Doors of Perception.*

"I suppose you tried all those things?" Amanda said.

Roger was astounded. Even to deny it seemed to accord more weight to her remark than he cared to. Did she imagine that he and Philip were children of the sixties, antinomian, reckless?

"You're thinking of Bridget."

Bridget Quirk was indeed, if she could be believed, a daughter of the sixties. She would roll her eyes and sigh over her *vita ante acta,* intimating that once she had lived with abandon, with no thought for the morrow.

"You never married, Bridget?"

"Oh, yes. One did, more or less."

Hans had told Roger of the husband who had disappeared. "Not a permanent commitment?"

Bridget gave him a look. It was not the past she wished to discuss with him. She had spoken with Roger about Amanda's dangerous excursions into lesser authors, meaning Chesterton. Roger sensed that defending Amanda on this matter would only make Bridget's censorious attitude indelible. But it was a sign of possible difficulties ahead. Roger wanted to think that others in the philosophy department would dismiss Bridget's misgivings. There must be one or two who had actually read Chesterton and would understand the interest. Still, he counseled Amanda to sin on the side of dullness until she received tenure.

Hans's strengths were his weaknesses so far as a tenure decision was concerned. The area in which he worked required a knowledge of French and German. Few of his authors were translated into English. This fact made the audience for his work narrow. The high praise he received had to be assessed by committee members who must accept on faith the credentials of those who praised the writings of Hans Wiener. Despite the recherché nature of his scholarly interests, he was an effective teacher. His survey of modern philosophy drew students in number, and his platform manner had earned him the epithet "Hot Dog." But the student evaluations of his teaching were, like the entrails of birds, susceptible of many interpretations.

In any sane world, it could be said, both these young people would be offered tenure at Notre Dame. In this vale of tears, given the roster of the department and the apportionment of tenured positions in the college, only one could be asked to stay.

11

was taken to Holy Cross House, where the papers that Henry Horan had given the university were stored, and was left to himself. "Lead us not into temptation," in the words of the Lord's Prayer, but here he was settling in for a stint in what must be regarded as the proximate occasion of sin. Or so he hoped. The purpose of his visit was about to be fulfilled.

He found himself in a windowless basement room, three of whose walls were poured concrete and the fourth, which contained the door through which he had come, of less permanent look. White-jacketed pipes were suspended from the ceiling, as were several fixtures containing flickering neon tubes that cast a lean and pale light on the trestle table on which three cartons had been placed by Whelan before he withdrew. They were standard archival boxes, indicating that the papers had been put into them after their arrival at Notre Dame.

Noah stood at the table and opened his hands in a priest-like way before setting to work. The next hour was spent on the first carton. Noah looked rapidly through the contents and assured himself that the object of his quest was not there. Dallying over what *was* there, interesting as it was, seemed to earn him the right to steal the Father Brown story when he found it. After finishing the first carton, he hesitated before drawing another toward him on the trestle table. Which one should be next? He moved them around on the surface as if they were walnut shells and he was a carnival con man trying to fool himself. The story was not in the second box he inspected. Finally,

he drew the third box toward him and laid his hands in benediction on its top. He was about to see the story that had
haunted Henry Horan's life, a youthful theft for which he had
been unable to compensate over the years and for which he had
never forgiven himself. The precedent was not encouraging.
Horan had wrongly taken possession of the story and it had
more or less ruined his life, or so at least he would have said.
Noah wondered about his own fate. But enough. He opened the
box and began to inspect its contents, first rapidly, then slowly,
then again very slowly and meticulously.

Astonishment gave way to bitter disappointment and then
to smoldering anger. The story was not there. He stared at the
box, but his mind was elsewhere. Vulgar words he had not used
in years formed on his lips and threatened to burst forth. Eventually, he calmed down. Review the facts. The story had been
given to Notre Dame. Noah was as sure of that as he was that a
man named Henry Horan had existed. Between its arrival on
campus and today someone had done what Noah had come to
South Bend to do. He closed the lid of the box and sat thinking
for a very long time. Who had beaten him to the punch? Who
had stolen the hitherto unpublished, because hitherto
unknown, Father Brown story?

There were several possibilities, the first already excluded
but logically possible: Horan had lied when he said in his diary
that he had included the Chesterton story in his gift to his alma
mater. Why would he lie to himself? There was no indication
that Horan had expected his diary to survive him, let alone be
read posthumously. He had made elaborate plans to destroy his
lifelong record of remorse, but he was taken before he could
fulfill that promise. No, Noah could not believe that the story
had not been among the papers Henry Horan had given to
Notre Dame. Having followed the anguish that story had caused
Horan through a long life, he was certain that, in the end, the
man's peace of mind could only be gained by giving up
the story.

On the assumption that Horan had given the story to Notre Dame, it should have been in one of these cartons, but it was clear that it was not to be found among the items in these three archival boxes. Then, of two things, one. The story had been put into one of the boxes and subsequently been removed. Or it had never been put among the items stored in the basement of Holy Cross House. In the latter case, Noah's suspicion turned to someone in the archives. The Horan papers had been boxed and put in storage by Whelan.

Noah looked around and saw an old wheelchair pushed into a corner of the basement room. It was difficult to move, as if the brake had stuck, but it was comfortable enough to sit in. The cracked leather of the seat received him as if it had been shaped to the national average bottom. The frame of the chair was steel tubing and one of the arms rests was missing. Noah folded his arms, closed his eyes, and thought about Whelan.

An archivist was in the same constant danger as a bank teller or someone working a payoff window at the track. To deal all day in money that was not one's own, money that belonged to others, did that really differ from spending one's day with historical treasures that were the property of the institution for which one worked? Had Whelan reached the point when he was no longer satisfied to spend his days among manuscripts and memorabilia of which he was the mere custodian? Surely a sense of proprietorship rose in the breast of the archivist as he worked on the items in his care. Did he resent patrons who came and demanded to see this or that, asses like Pottery, with their imperious manner, as if they owned what they wanted to inspect? No doubt, no doubt, but Noah had trouble imagining Whelan spiriting anything out of the archives. It would have contradicted his whole life. If Horan had been riddled with guilt, Whelan would have been undone by such perfidy.

Besides, Whelan had given Noah permission to check out the boxes in storage. If he had come upon the Father Brown story and removed it, he would wonder if it really was as secret as it seemed. He would have thought of the diary Noah owned, and his guilt would have prompted him to think that Noah knew what should be in those boxes. And in that case, he would wonder if Noah intended to steal the story. Looked at in that light, Noah's generosity to the archives would appear for what it was, a screen. No, it seemed unlikely that Whelan had discovered the story, taken it, and then provided Noah with the opportunity of discovering what he had done. Possible, perhaps, but unlikely.

The other possibility was that someone passionately interested in Chesterton had been unwilling to wait for the papers to be processed by the archives and, having learned where they were stored, had gone through them. Noah knew that Roger Knight had been allowed to look at the Horan bequest. But it was impossible to think of the portly professor purloining the story, at least the portly professor that Roger was. Sean Pottery? Noah had no difficulty imagining the pompous professor of English assuming that he had a divine right to examine the papers. And, of course, he would understand the importance of an unpublished Father Brown story. Could he have resisted taking such a prize?

But this line of thought was pushed aside as the image of Amanda Pick formed in his mind. Amanda. She was a young woman animated by the zeal of the amateur. But no, the image faded. He could not believe her capable of such a theft.

But someone had taken that story.

12

to a slice of raisin toast, Philip looked across the breakfast table at his brother, Roger, and beamed.

"Basketball tonight."

"Good."

"We can have an early dinner at the University Club and go from there."

"Walk?"

"I'll take the golf cart over earlier. We can park in the club lot, take the cart to the ACC, and then come back for the car."

It was pleasant to think that Philip had nothing more demanding to take care of than the logistics of dinner and transport to a basketball game. On the other hand, Roger had no wish to see his brother atrophy. It had been some little while since Philip had accepted a client. A tempting call from Denver involving an apparently disappeared husband had caused him to waver, but in the end he'd decided he could not be absent from the opening home game of the basketball season. Philip might be one of the few fans who was unequivocally in favor of the Irish membership in the Big East, and he'd waved away Roger's remarks about the geographical anomalies of the association. How could an Indiana team be classified as eastern?

"Notre Dame is a national team, Roger."

"A transcendental entity?"

"If you say so."

"Then it is better to be independent of regional associations."

But neither brother was really that committed to one view or another. For Philip, the great bonus of Roger's move to Notre Dame was that he had apparent nonstop access to first-rate athletic events. Later, Roger checked his E-mail and the phone messages, half hoping that some irresistible case would come Philip's way. He was half relieved when there were none.

Roger himself, as he settled down at his computer, found himself reflecting on how complicated life was just beneath the apparently placid surface of academe. So many of his new friends and acquaintances on campus were confronting anguishing situations. When he realized that Amanda was actually facing the prospect of being denied tenure, and realizing that then she must soon leave the campus forever, he was filled with a great sadness. It was not only that he knew how much she wanted to stay and how perfectly she seemed to him to fit into the Notre Dame faculty, there was also the grim reality that finding a comparable job after being denied tenure here was all but impossible. If she remained in teaching, it would be at a considerably less prestigious and interesting level.

How did she stand it? Weeks ago he had been able to discuss the matter with Sean Pottery, but now the bibulous infatuation of the professor of English had made him an enemy of Amanda, at least when he was sober. He had embarrassed himself with her, and he irrationally blamed her for his lapse. Roger had heard that he had pooh-poohed her work on Chesterton, which was surely unjust. So Roger made the demanding trip to Decio and rose in the protesting elevator to Pottery's office.

The door was open. Within was a chaos of books and papers and tobacco smoke and the ceaseless rumble of the professorial voice. But when Roger looked in, the great man was seated at his desk, hands folded on his paunch, eyes closed, lips tight. Was he a ventriloquist? And then Roger noted the light on the cassette player. He had surprised Pottery listening with great attentiveness to a recording of one of his own lectures. Is it possible to interrupt a past event? Roger knocked.

A hand went up, the eyes remaining closed. A minute later, after a grand peroration, the tape ended and Pottery opened his eyes. He looked at Roger with an expression somewhere between surprise and wariness. "I had to listen to that before authorizing its distribution."

"I must get a copy."

Pottery cleared his throat but did not comment. Roger knew that there was a far-flung army of Pottery admirers among the alumni and that it was to satisfy their craving for the remembrance of things past that a newsletter, a web page, and such recordings as Pottery had just played had been devised.

"Have you ever been to Wheaton College, Professor Pottery?"

"Criminal, sir. Absolutely criminal."

He explained himself in great looping sentences. The little evangelical college near Chicago had ended up as the repository of the papers of C. S. Lewis and other Inklings (fair enough, perhaps) but also of some Chesterton things. That Notre Dame had permitted such treasures to slip into the hands of—well, in this ecumenical age one cannot characterize the enemies of the faith as once one could. Nonetheless . . .

Roger took the proffered chair and let Pottery run through what seemed to be, at least in part, standard repertoire. It was the professor's conceit that he and he alone understood the nature and obligations of the University of Notre Dame, a lonely status that doomed him to be the witness of one betrayal of that tradition after another. The Newman holdings might have been cited as balance to the Chesterton complaint—and, after all, what Wheaton had of Chesterton was a complete bound edition of *G.K.'s Weekly*, precious but not without its counterpart. A veritable display of fireworks might have been let loose if Roger had broached the subject of the Ignatius Press Chesterton. That a publisher had had the effrontery to launch such an edition without receiving the Pottery imprimatur was not to be suffered. But there were fireworks enough without heat, and listening to the volcanic eruption of pomposity, Roger tried to imagine the professor helplessly, if drunkenly, falling at the feet of Amanda Pick. *In vino veritas*, in the old saying. That Pottery's public persona was a pose, having little to do with his inner self, was an attractive thought.

"Amanda Pick is worried about her tenure decision," he said in a lull.

"The decision is not hers."

"She fears it could go against her."

"Is this public knowledge?"

"I have come to know her slightly."

A bloodshot eye scanned Roger and then dismissed him as a possible rival.

"She should have stuck to her last."

"And stayed away from Chesterton?"

"I can scarcely be expected to discourage interest in Gilbert Chesterton, but she presumed to wander into an academic field other than her own."

"That makes her sound Chestertonian."

A pause. "Perhaps. But then Chesterton did not have to gain tenure in what universities have become."

"She feels that Cheval and Quirk are opposed to her."

"Has she spoken to them about it?"

"Good heavens, no."

"That would have been fatal."

"Could someone else speak to them on her behalf."

Again the bloodshot eye scanned Roger. "You?"

"I was thinking of you. They would respect your opinion."

"I flatter myself that they would. But Professor Knight, if you think I could characterize her work on Chesterton as sufficient to overcome her scholarly deficiencies in her own field, well . . ."

"I have read her work with interest."

"As have I."

"Of course I am an amateur."

70

"Exactly! As is she! *Sub specie aeternitatis*, amateur status, may be infinitely more pleasing to God and doubtless to Gilbert Chesterton as well; but when it comes to a tenure committee at the ragtag end of the second millennium, I am afraid that to be an amateur is to be a dilettante."

Doubtless there was something sincere in what Pottery said, but it was noteworthy that he insisted on a distance between himself and the criteria that would very well work against Amanda's hopes for tenure. There were scholars who would classify Pottery as a heightened amateur, but then that same scholarly class had been disdainful of Chesterton and had been answered masterfully by Hilaire Belloc.

> *Remote and ineffectual Don*
> *That dared attack my Chesterton,*
> *With that poor weapon, half-impelled,*
> *Unlearnt, unsteady, hardly held,*
> *Unworthy for a tilt with men—*
> *Your quavering and corroded pen;*
> *Don poor at bed and worse at table,*
> *Don pinched, Don starved, Don miserable;*
> *Don stuttering, Don with roving eyes,*
> *Don nervous, Don of crudities . . .*

And so on, until Chesterton's critics were pulverized. But Roger rejected the similarity. He decided that there was nothing truly Chestertonian about Pottery the man. He was proving himself to be a vindictive, unrequited lover, willing to see Amanda's career blighted because she had prompted his lapse into common humanity.

"Sometimes I almost envy her the prospect of being turned down for tenure," Laura said to Roger, when they met to talk about her housemate.

"Envy her?"

"A new start, just leave all this and begin again somewhere else, a new place, new friends . . . "

Laura might have been thinking of her failed marriage and her importunate husband rather than of academe, but she did not sound as if she meant what she said. Was she rehearsing consoling speeches to make if things did indeed go badly for Amanda?

"Professor Pottery won't help."

"You talked to him about Amanda?"

Roger gave her an account of the talk he had had with Pottery in the professor's Decio office.

"Amanda must have told you what is really going on there."

"I must say he looks harmless enough in his office."

"And he is. That isn't the point. These episodes cannot simply be wished away. There are now large numbers of women on university faculties, but still some of the old condescension remains. Only if it is punished when it comes to light will the future be what it ought to be for women professors."

Roger had been told by Whelan that Laura and Professor Pottery had been drinking in a bar near his apartment, a fact the archivist discovered when, unable to sleep, he had dressed and gone out for a postmidnight drink. His surprising description of Laura and Pottery was of an amorous couple.

"The mother bird feigning injury to lure the predator away from the nest."

But Whelan had only shrugged at this explanation. Meanwhile it was clear that Noah Beispiel was fascinated by Amanda. Several times, when Roger had been looking forward to lunch with Amanda, she had gone off with the rare book dealer. All the more reason for delight when she looked into his carrel and asked Roger in an excited voice if he were free for lunch.

That was when she told him of her incredible discovery.

13

dence among regulars in the archives, and Noah was reminded of the legend he had seen embroidered on a pillow in a pricey store in Palm Beach: I never repeat gossip, so listen carefully. When the news came to him, it had an obviousness and inevitability about it that made him think he had known it all along. Of course.

"Perhaps this will make the difference in her tenure decision," Roger said.

Noah explored this possibility with the obese Huneker Professor and rang the changes on the unlikelihood of such a discovery. "There is no doubt of its authenticity?"

"That is why I have come to you."

Noah's heart was in his throat when Roger opened his book bag and pulled out a sheaf of papers. It was all Noah could do not to snatch them from Roger, but the papers were put immediately into his hands.

"She made a copy for me."

Noah had seen immediately that what Roger had given him was a photocopy. These were not the circumstances in which he had imagined himself perusing the story of which he had read so much in the diaries of Henry Horan. If he himself had found it, he too might have photocopied it after first examining the manuscript with a dealer's eye. The story as story could be enjoyed as well in a copy as in the original. Amanda had wisely kept the original from circulation. He did not have to go past the first page to be certain that this was indeed a story from the hand of Gilbert Keith Chesterton. Noah almost felt gratitude to Amanda for showing such consideration to a manuscript that he considered rightfully his own. And eventually it would be his own. But it was not gratitude he felt but resentment, anger, hatred. He felt that his birthright had been claimed by another.

"No doubt about its genuineness."

"My judgment exactly. Of course I am only an amateur."

"Has Professor Pottery been shown this story."

"He mustn't even know of it!"

"But his judgment . . . "

"His mind is clouded when it comes to Amanda." Roger hesitated, looked over Noah's shoulder, looked into his eyes, and then leaned toward him. "So listen carefully."

14

were located on the sixth floor of Hesburgh Library and had been since 1963 when the library first opened. Nonetheless, these were temporary quarters; the space was meant for general library use and was therefore coveted by the librarian. This was not unequivocally bad news for the archives, since once the building plans for an archive building were approved and added to the construction queue, serious plans for transferring all the archival treasures to that new setting would get under way. This impending contingency added poignancy to the task of retaining the records of the past.

Greg Whelan, a shy man with doctorates in both English and law, had finally come to port in a subordinate position in the archives and had settled among the cartons and cases and cabinets with a sense of having reached his personal promised land. The only negative aspect of his job was having to deal with some of the scholars who came to work on materials. These were the officious types who spoke too loudly and treated Whelan as if he were a mere librarian. His damnable stammer kept him silent during the indignities he often suffered. No indignities could match those he suffered whenever Prof. Sean Pottery swept into the archives, for all the world as if they had been awaiting him and wanted nothing better than to jump at his imperious commands. But he was particularly obnoxious when he arrived after the supposedly still secret discovery of a Father Brown story among the Horan papers.

"Chesterton!" he cried, as he wrestled with his overcoat. "Give me a list of everything we have of Chesterton."

"Whelan," said the head archivist, and Whelan nodded.

He went off without a word, as much to get out of sight of the obnoxious professor as to do his bidding. He came upon Amanda ensconced behind a file cabinet in an inner room. She brought a finger to her lips.

"I didn't know you were here." To his surprise, he managed to enunciate this sentence without trouble.

"Is that Professor Pottery out there?" Whelan made a face as he nodded, and she went on in a whisper. "What does he want?"

Whelan printed "Everything on Chesterton" on a pad and showed it to her. She reacted as if he had struck her. He took her elbow and led her back among the cartons and boxes to his work area. They might have been coconspirators. Although she did not know it, Whelan was in greater potential trouble than the assistant professor. After all, he had colluded with her in spiriting her great discovery from the archives, thereby violating every aspect of the archivist's moral code. It would not have done to make a copy on the archives' machine, lest someone wander by and see what she was doing.

"I won't stamp it University of Notre Dame Archives until you return it."

Photocopiers would balk at accepting such a document with the university seal on it. Whelan had anticipated her hope that the discovery was her ticket to tenure and a permanent appointment at Notre Dame. Indeed, it was Whelan who had first corroborated her guess that she had stumbled onto a Father Brown story written by Chesterton at Notre Dame when the English author was a visiting professor.

It was a secret known but to God that Whelan had first become aware of the possible Chesterton story while putting into order materials recording the history of the *Scholastic*, once the publication of record of the university. He found it easy to be enthralled by any period of the institution and was particularly susceptible to the evocative power of ancient issues of the publication. It had been the general belief that the history of the *Scholastic* was all but identical with the printed issues of the magazine, but Whelan had come upon a trove of hitherto uncatalogued papers that proved to be editorial records of the late 1920s and early 1930s. One standard for arranging undated materials was the journal itself, and when he approached the year 1931 and read the printed accounts of the visit of Chesterton to the campus and the great success his lectures in Washington Hall had been, he could not help wondering if there was any correspondence between the great man and the then editorial staff of the *Scholastic.* When he found a scrawled note in the distinctive hand promising a story for the *Scholastic,* Whelan's research became even more intense, but he had been unsuccessful—until the Henry Horan papers came in. While transferring them to archival boxes, he came upon the handwritten original of "Star of the Sea," a Father Brown story.

It was Whelan's cross that his tongue refused to serve his mind, at least in the presence of others. As often as not, when he spoke in public his stutter would render him silent and his addressee would turn away embarrassed. Perhaps if he had not been so afflicted, he would have run shouting through the archives announcing his discovery. Of course he did not. And soon caution returned. It became clear that among the tributes paid to Chesterton during his visit had been conducting a contest to see what student could most closely ape the great writer's style. Whelan turned up three such imitations among the *Scholastic* editorial correspondence, and had no difficulty seeing that they were imitations. But "Star of the Sea" was the genuine article; he was sure of it.

Some days later, Amanda Pick's presence in the archives made Whelan think that she was the reason he still had not announced his discovery, guarding the secret as if the discovery was merely phase one of an unfolding drama. It was when Roger Knight broached the topic of Chesterton one day when the three of them were having coffee in the library pit that a great idea formed in Whelan's mind. It only strengthened as time went on. Amanda had become a regular user of the archives, also a favorite place of Roger Knight's, and the two of them were drawn together by a mutual love of Chesterton. Amanda's main reason for coming to the archives was Chesterton; she had written a nice piece on Chesterton's series of lectures on Victorian literature.

"Someone should reissue his little book on Dickens," Amanda enthused. Roger Knight agreed with her high estimate of the book. Now Amanda was studying the impact Chesterton had had on students. She would learn of the Chesterton imitation contest. It was only a matter of time before he offhandedly suggested that it might be worth her while to check out the contemporary records of Chesterton's visit in the *Scholastic*.

"Are there any nonprinted materials?"

"I'll look."

He'd felt almost godlike, arranging things so that she might freely discover what he knew was there. But a full week went by before Amanda asked Whelan to come with her for coffee. Her manner told him what was afoot. But she approached the matter cautiously, going on about what she had learned of Chesterton's visit, his lectures, his legendary capacity for alcohol. Would she never come upon the manuscript Whelan had withheld from the Horan boxes, putting it among the *Scholastic* materials so that Amanda would find it?

Whelan said offhandedly, "There was a contest at the time to see if a student could imitate Chesterton's style."

"I've come upon that."

"Now, if you've found some imitation Chesterton . . . "

"Yes." A silence. She looked into his eyes, as if debating whether to go on. And then she did, leaning toward him and putting her hand on his. "I found a genuine Chesterton story, too."

Her main concern was that his reaction not be one of skepticism, and she did not detect that her announcement did not come as news to him. Assured that he was a receptive audience, she went excitedly on. He was momentarily taken aback when she told him she had already confided her discovery in Roger Knight.

"Greg, if I'm right, this just might get me tenure."

In responding to Pottery's request two weeks later, Whelan provided the professor with everything in the archives listed under the name of Chesterton. He felt no obligation to mention the *Scholastic* materials.

"This is everything?" Pottery asked, as he glanced over the printout Whelan had handed him.

"You can do a search on the computer as well." Whelan emitted each word with difficulty, but managed to get out the complete sentence. Pottery looked at him sharply. "Didn't you already do that?"

Whelan nodded, not wanting to risk another sentence. He indicated that the printout Pottery held was the result of his own search.

"You mean I can second-guess you?"

A moment went by before Pottery laughed.

15

script was of such high resolution that Amanda felt she had kept the original when she examined the Chesterton story at home. Thus far, she had told only Roger and Whelan. She felt foolish at the way she had blurted out to the archivist her great discovery. It would not have been fair to exclude the archivist from this historic event. Still, it seemed right that she had told Roger first. Whelan was sympathetic and congenial, perhaps more, and that was what made her uneasy about the archivist. Too often she surprised his wistful eyes upon her when she turned from her desk in the archives. Not that he was a nuisance or anything remotely like it, but Amanda did not want to encourage anything more than a professional link with him. Pottery had been trouble enough in that regard.

Step one in testing her find had been to consult the four collections of Father Brown stories that Chesterton had published. Amanda had them all in a single jumbo volume. *The Father Brown Omnibus.* She had bought it on a foray to Casperson's bookstore in Niles.

"That is the edition in which I first read him," Roger said with feeling. He tested the heft of the book, turned it in his hands, ran his fingers over its green cover. Amanda began to fear that Roger would ask to buy the book for himself. She actually offered to let him have it.

"Oh, I already own it."

"The copy you read when you were a boy?"

"Yes."

His love of Chesterton was only one of the bonuses of Roger's friendship. How flattering it was to have so eminent a senior member of the faculty for a friend—without fear of emotional complications. The senior endowed professors in her own department, Horace Cheval and Bridget Quirk, treated her civilly, but Amanda always felt that they regarded her presence as threatening. Not because of her teaching or publications, God knows; it was youth they resented, hers and Hans Wiener's, too. If only they had the same cordiality Roger had, her thoughts about her future at Notre Dame would have been considerably different.

When Amanda made her great discovery it was at first difficult to say whether it was a plus or minus in her quest for tenure. Roger counseled silence until her find had been authenticated. "I believe it is authentic, Amanda."

She could have hugged him for being so certain. "I am so anxious to know what effect it will have on my chances for tenure."

"I could bring it up with Horace Cheval."

She squeezed his hand. "Would you?"

16

Chicago with Bridget Quirk, who was not returning directly to
South Bend from the regional philosophy meeting.

"There should be someone else you can come back with."

That sounded iffy but he didn't want to leave Teresa without a car, so he took a chance on it. The atmosphere of a meeting is not conducive to philosophical thought, at least of the
consoling sort. There were so many good papers being read and
such a surfeit of bright and confident young people that one
would not have guessed how parlous was the job situation that
confronted them all. Hans was reminded forcibly of the meeting half a dozen years before at which he had been interviewed
by the Notre Dame delegation. That had led to the on-campus
interview and his eventual employment. Yet here he was six
years later, not really certain that the tenure decision would go
in his favor. If not, in a year he would be desperately looking
for another job, but with the negative cloud of not having
received tenure at Notre Dame hanging over him.

He read a paper on Lyotard in a small room with only a
dozen in the audience, but they made up in interest what they
lacked in numbers. The discussion threatened to go on into
the next scheduled talk and it seemed reluctantly that they
broke up.

"Let me buy you a drink," said a bearded fellow who had
pressed him hard for ten minutes and had seemed convinced
against his will of Hans's point. He wanted to continue the discussion over a beer.

His name was Strawler, he was chair of a department at one of the California campuses, and he told Hans that he had never heard a better paper on Lyotard in his life. "You blew all of my own theories out of the water."

And then it dawned on Hans that this was the Strawler whose work he knew and admired. It was pleasant to be able to return the compliment. They were on a second beer when Horst came in. He seemed to have been looking for Hans, but when he saw he was with someone he made a gesture and was about to withdraw. It seemed too good a chance to have his chair listen to high praise of his paper from another philosopher. Hans insisted that Horst join them.

"I wondered if you had a ride back to South Bend."

"When are you leaving?"

That settled, he introduced Horst to Strawler, whom Horst did not know except by name. He went on a bit about some of the people in Strawler's department. Strawler agreed that his was a good department. But he added, "I think you have a better man in Contemporary Continental."

Strawler repeated some of his earlier praise, and when they broke up and Hans and Horst headed out to the chair's car, Hans felt that his tenure prospects had just received a powerful boost. But any elation he felt was dissipated during the drive home. Horst told Hans that it was no small thing to have made such an impression on Strawler.

"I have this in confidence, Hans. They will be interviewing this year. All they need is a go ahead from the chancellor."

"What are they looking for?"

"The job description could have been written with you in mind."

Hans let that go and tried to get Horst to talk about the panel he had been on, but the chair returned to Strawler. "Hans, I'm completely off base asking this and tell me to go to hell if you like, but did he tell you about their position?"

Hans hesitated. To say no might seem to negate all the

praise Strawler had heaped on him. To say yes would be a lie. "That's not a question I want to answer."

"Absolutely. I understand." Horst waved the topic away, but it was clear what he thought that answer meant. They talked of other things, but when signs announced the South Bend exit, Horst said, "Look, I've already broken a number of rules. Let me break another. Hans, the way things look on the Appointments and Promotion Committee, I wouldn't discourage Stawler's interest."

"You wouldn't?"

"Don't ask me to enlarge on it. But a word to the wise . . . "

At home, he tried to tell Teresa of the meeting, but what had been the great news of Strawler's praise was now bracketed in his mind with Horst's hint that Hans was not going to get tenure. It was small consolation to think that, but for those indiscreet remarks of Horst's, he would have gone on hoping to receive tenure at Notre Dame. Now he had it from the horse's mouth, Horst himself, that his chances were next to nil. That meant the nod would go to Amanda Pick.

A deep sense of the injustice of that choice flooded through Hans. Here he was, the better philosopher by any objective estimate, a man with large obligations besides, Teresa and the kids, and he would get the heave-ho while Amanda stayed. He had heard that she was the darling of senior professors, not just Roger Knight but of Sean Pottery as well. Hans raked over in his mind the trip to Chicago with Bridget to see if she had given any hint as to which direction her judgment leaned. It would be her judgment and Horace Cheval's that would matter. What had Bridget said when they were exchanging compliments of Amanda? "Horace tells me she has made some *literary* discovery." Her tone had been ironic and she had italicized literary. He would have taken comfort from the implications of her tone, and Strawler's praise had been a tonic, but Horst's indiscreet confidence was such a downer that he had almost forgotten the remark. What did that mean, a "*literary* discovery."

The following day Hans looked in on Roger Knight. After some preliminary pleasantries, he asked, "What's this about Amanda's literary discovery?"

Roger seemed astounded. "Did she tell you?"

"Word's around," Hans managed to say and got out of there. In his own office, he sat staring out at the campus. Clouds heavy with the promise of snow hung over the stadium. His hands gripped the arms of his chair so tightly his knuckles were white. It wasn't fair. He had triumphed in Chicago with his Lyotard paper, and it wouldn't matter at all. He brought his fist down on the surface of his desk with a loud bang, causing books to topple and paper clips to dance.

if he were counting, and snorted with displeasure. "It is a work of fiction," he said to Bridget, "a short story."

The two senior philosophers had doubtless in their remote pasts read a novel or two, but they had long since put away the things of a child and devoted their minds to more worthy objects. Why anyone would devote time to reading about the antics of imaginary human agents was beyond their comprehension. From time to time there had been members of the department who put works of fiction on the reading lists for their classes, arguing that Dostoyevsky provided a better basis for discussion than, say, Gilbert Ryle. These people had been denied tenure, largely because of the opposition of Cheval and Bridget. The two senior professors had come to form a surprising alliance against the forces of unreason. Bridget's passion was Leibniz, Cheval's Plato. They had little in common except seniority and the conviction that the mind was in an advanced state of atrophy among other members of the department. They sat now over stout in the back bar of the University Club reeling under this new development.

"Roger told me of it as if it were a scholarly achievement."

"Dear God."

"It is a detective story by Chesterton."

Bridget shook her head. She knew no one of that name.

"A Father Brown story."

"Father Brown?"

"The sleuth is a Catholic priest."

Remote as the memory of innocence was the faith of Bridget's fathers. She had not apostosized; there had been no dramatic break with the faith. Catholicism had simply faded from her mind. This would doubtless seem strange to someone like Roger, for whom the campus contained a hundred reminders of its religious origins and its continued role as the premier Catholic university in the land. But familiarity had worked its usual effect on Bridget and she found Roger's enthusiasm naïve.

"If he is this impressed with the green wood, what would he have made of the dry?"

Bridget frowned, her expression indicating that she suspected a quote, her silence betraying the fact that she did not recognize it. What had Allan Bloom said of the scriptural illiteracy of undergraduates? Cheval thought that he should have quizzed the faculty. *Et tu,* Bridget?

"Roger tells you that it is authentic? She will be famous."

"With whom?" Cheval harumphed. "She may become a laughing stock. Pottery assures me that the story cannot be authentic."

"Pottery? Well, well. Chesterfield is his bailiwick, is it not?"

"Chesterton. He is an acknowledged expert."

"Well, then."

Bridget cleared her throat and allowed some moments to pass. "Horace, if she were to come under a cloud, that does not mean that the sun must shine on him."

Cheval, of course, understood the reference of these pronouns. He assumed an enigmatic expression. Had Bridget conveyed to Horst the difficulties facing Hans Weiner as a tenure prospect? The principal obstacle was her unwillingness to have another tenured male in the department. Let her continue to think that Amanda had a champion in himself, but he had listened long to Pottery's judgment of her.

"I thought you were quite taken with her, Sean?"

"What do you mean?"

"Only what I said."

"I will not have insinuations made about my personal life."

"It never entered my head."

"You may hear rumors. Discount them, Horace. We are all subject to libel."

He would not definitely assure Pottery that the young colleague who seemed lately to have earned his animosity would not have her prospects enhanced as a result of discovering a lost piece of fiction. Certitude on the matter eluded him. But there was danger here. The administration lusted after notoriety, and any notice taken of a faculty member for anything short of moral turpitude gladdened the administrative breast. A young person brought into the public eye, even for something as irrelevant as this detective story, would be very difficult to keep from admission to the tenured faculty.

"Bopp," Cheval muttered.

"Bopp," Quirk repeated.

Maurice Bopp was a young man who, while a talented philosopher, had become a hit on the circuit of alumni clubs. Soon he was a favorite from coast to coast. Demands for his appearance multiplied from alumni groups across the land. His publications were minimal but because of his popularity, however irrelevant to the academic life, it had been impossible to refuse him tenure. The administration would have overruled a negative vote by the department, an unthinkable reversal. Snookered, they had voted to award Bopp tenure. Two years later he had left the academic life to devote himself exclusively to what he called "motivational speaking," an occupation in which, to quote Bopp himself, he was literally coining money. Once he had lectured eloquently on the impossibility of finding happiness in wealth; now he was in relentless pursuit of the dollar. The man remained as a moral lesson for the department.

Neither Cheval nor Quirk intended to repeat the blunder they had made with Bopp.

"And what of Wiener?" Bridget asked. It was one thing to acknowledge that the female candidate could not expect to gain tenure on the basis of her discovery of a hitherto unknown detective story by Chesterton, but quite another to waive all objections to the male candidate.

"I thought we were agreed that it was one or the other."

"I think what we were agreed upon is that we have one position and two candidates."

"Exactly. One of whom seems to fall short of the requirements for tenure."

"As the other might also do."

"Meaning neither of them is offered tenure?" It would perhaps be unfair to say that the prospect of disappointing both Amanda and Hans brought a spark of pleasure to the eye of Horace Cheval. The unsuccessful candidate for tenure was carried on the faculty for another year, during which time he or she could seek employment elsewhere. A negative decision on both candidates would give the department as well as the candidates a year of grace. The great decision of offering tenure could be put off until the following year, a search could be initiated, much time and thought would have to be given to the next move. They might bring in replacements for Amanda and Hans, replacements who would not be eligible for tenure until six long years had passed. But this inviting prospect of freedom had its pitfalls. Horace thought he detected a gleam in Bridget's eye. Did his senior colleague see opportunities for affirmative action claims in the future if both Amanda and Hans fell by the wayside? Did she perhaps imagine that she might be able to replace both of them with women, thus tipping the balance of the department in the direction of those for whom gender in all its many valences was a primary concern?

Horace made the pensive noise his enemies described as a whinny.

"I am not sure the departmental committee has allowed that much discretion."

"I thought we were talking as the ad hoc committee of endowed professors in the department."

Above the traditional rank of full professor was that of the endowed professorship, analogous to the five-star general who had been placed above the hitherto supreme four-star rank. Both Horace and Bridget had long since ascended into the heady stratosphere, and it was in that rarefied atmosphere that they had entered into discussions of the fate of Amanda and Hans. For Horace to bring in the departmental committee had the suggestion of the Supreme Court appealing to a lower court.

"Of course." Where did Roger Knight stand on the two young people? Roger was arguably a member of the department. As Huneker professor he transcended the usual departmental divisions, but his courses were usually cross-listed in philosophy. Horace wondered if it might not be feasible to take counsel with Roger and enlist his support. Working with Bridget alone demanded either agreement or impasse.

"Pottery dismisses the very possibility of Amanda's discovery being genuine."

"You consulted him?"

"You could call it that."

Surely Pottery's dismissal of the very possibility of the story being genuine was reason enough for Horace to go back to Roger with the matter. He considered himself to have carte blanche to approach Roger without any need to forewarn Bridget that he meant to do so. How much more pleasant it would be to pursue these matters if he sat down with a proxy vote besides his own, thus outweighing Bridget from the outset. All things being equal, Horace wanted Hans to be offered tenure. Bridget's negative attitude toward Amanda, on the basis of the young woman's incredible interest in popular literature, might be construed as welcome only because it opened the way to securing tenure for Hans. Putting off the evil day, starting anew a year from now with two junior appointments, was attractive only on the assumption that he would be the determining factor in those future tenure decisions. But now was now, and to ensure that Hans would be permanently a colleague had all the attractions of the proximately possible. A bird in the hand, as it were.

The following morning, Professor Cheval was in his office at seven. The early hours of the day were the most productive, and Decio was quiet as a tomb. Younger faculty worked at home, if at all, and in any case were not early risers. Cheval counted on uninterrupted quiet, and that is what he usually had. Therefore, when his telephone rang, he lurched back and glared at it. He would have ignored it if it did not continue to ring. He snatched it up and growled hello.

"This is Manfred in the office."

"Manfred?"

"The student assistant."

"What is it?"

"I'm calling everyone. Her body was found in the lake this morning."

"What are you talking about."

"Amanda Pick. She's dead. Someone discovered her body in the lake."

PART TWO

AFTER

18

north shore of Saint Joseph's Lake on Douglas Road, just east of Moreau Seminary, where aspiring members of the congregation begin their long years of study. After ordination they are assigned to various posts throughout the country, indeed throughout the world. Only a small fraction join the faculty or administration of Notre Dame, the jewel in the crown of the Congregation of Holy Cross. But wherever their active priestly lives are led, members are likely to end where they began and spend their twilight time in Holy Cross House at Notre Dame. Younger men referred to it lightheartedly as "the terminal," but with age they began to regard the place with unease and then with active dislike. In any case, eventually, each would lie beneath an identical cross in the community cemetery, situated in the northwest corner of the campus, but that common posthumous destination affected the imagination less strongly than the sight of the building in which one would likely ail, perhaps feel pain, eventually slip away, toothless, hairless, to be mourned perfunctorily and soon forgotten by all save God.

The view from within the house was, of course, different. Just as no one thinks of himself as the average man, so no inhabitant of Holy Cross House thought of himself, while thought was still possible, as in the same condition as any of the others. There was no one of whom this was truer than Fr. Matthew Rush. Still mobile, he prowled the halls in baggy corduroys and sweatshirt, a baseball cap pulled low over eyes renewed by laser surgery, making swift and condescending visits to the bedridden. In chapel, he liked to be the principal celebrant. His reason, never voiced, was less than edifying. If he was to drink from a common cup at Communion, he wanted to be the first to lift it to his lips. God only knew what viral oddities and potential infirmities might later lurk on the chalice rim. This fear diminished in no way his profound belief in and reverence toward Jesus sacramentally present under the appearance of wine.

The community mass was celebrated in the afternoon, at four-thirty, and Father Rush had spent his priestly years offering his mass at the crack of dawn. His attempt during his first days at Holy Cross House to say an early morning private mass met with adamant opposition on the part of young Arundel, the chaplain.

"The mass is a meal, Father, not a snack. What is the point of dining alone?"

"Are you saying it wouldn't be valid?" Young priests had a way of suggesting that everything had been redefined by Vatican II. Father Rush had no clear memories of the council, but these young pups had not even been weaned while it was going on.

"It's not a question of validity," Arundel said, pronouncing the word in descending, dirgelike notes.

It wasn't so much that Arundel won the argument, as that Father Rush found the sacristy locked and no one with a key when he crept down to the chapel the following morning. He reconciled himself to the community mass and the perils of the common cup. But he still awoke with the birds. He said his morning office by lamplight in winter then paced the parking lot for ten brisk minutes before sitting on a bench that overlooked the lake and gave a view of the golden dome and the spire of Sacred Heart Basilica, two sights that Father Rush had kept vivid in his memory during his long years in Bangladesh. Every morning, like clockwork, the lady jogger came along the path. Father Rush knew that she would go twice around the lake.

This morning, puzzled by something half visible in the shallow waters below, Father Rush had sat with clenched fists as the jogging woman came into sight, willing her to notice, but she puffed on past—the first time. The second time, his prayer was answered. She stopped, she went closer, she bent forward and then seemed to test the waters with the toe of her sneaker. Her mouth opened as if to emit a primal scream but time passed before the shrill sound of her screaming lifted ducks from the lake and caused a twittering riot among the wrens and sparrows and robins within earshot.

Father Rush settled back on his bench. The time before breakfast now promised to be more eventful than usual. The arrival of official vehicles confirmed his hunch and when Father Carmody became visible, Father Rush was certain that a drama was about to unfold.

19

through the university, much as it would have in the nineteenth century, that is, by word of mouth. True, mouths could now use telephones, but countless individual calls were needed to pass on the horrible news. Clotilde, the secretary of the philosophy department, thinking the call was a joke being played by a graduate student who had been up too late, or perhaps gotten up too early, hung up on the associate dean. The campus paper had already gone to press, the student FM stations continued their taped programming, which, at this early hour of the morning, had few listeners. Eventually Clotilde accepted the call and the dreadful news. She gave Manfred, the student assistant, the task of informing the faculty. At this hour, it would be a wake-up call for many, and the faculty could be surly at the best of times. Let Manfred handle it.

Some hours later, vice presidents, assistant and associate provosts, administrative assistants and their staffs, a veritable army of second violinists, had been assembled in the main building.

"Was it suicide?"

"That hasn't been determined."

"Who exactly was she?"

"Amanda Pick?"

Amanda Pick was located in the campus directory; the appropriate page of the photo directory was found and passed from hand to hand. Small intimations of mortality teased the minds of those around the table but were shrugged away. A working disbelief in one's own eventual death is a condition of life.

"Why do people insist on wearing dark glasses when they are being photographed?"

"She's not wearing dark glasses."

"It was a general question."

"She was up for tenure this year." Father Finn, a small man with wild hair, was reading from a folder that an aide to his assistant had brought in. The remark earned a moment of silence.

"Was she likely to get it?"

"Only the departmental committee would know for sure."

"Aren't their proceedings confidential?"

A hand raked through the wild hair, making it wilder. "This office has a right to the relevant information."

A stern young female looked up from the manila folder whose contents she had been perusing. "She had filed a sexual harassment suit against a senior colleague."

"Who is he?"

"My God!" Finn cried. "Don't answer that question." He took possession of the manila folder. "I warned against setting up an office to handle such matters. It only encourages complaints." Meanwhile he rapidly scanned the contents of the folder, after which he handed it to Father Carmody.

"I have a suggestion," said Father Carmody, after noting the item Finn brought to his attention. It was Carmody who had brought the news to Finn that a body had been discovered in the lake, and it was Carmody who had been asked to stay for the meeting. The older priest's tone was oil upon the waters of gathering rancor. "Of course we do not yet know what is involved here. It may or may not prove to be sticky. Nonetheless, it would be prudent to bring in someone to represent us on this matter."

"A lawyer!"

"Oh, I think we have enough lawyers as it is. I meant a private investigator."

"Ah."

Anxiety subsided, coffee cups were refilled, one might have thought the purpose of the meeting had been achieved. And, given the expression on Father Carmody's face, perhaps it had been.

"Do you have someone in mind, Father Carmody?"

"I do. Philip Knight."

Finn paused and then nodded, not quite smiling. "Will you take care of it?"

"If you wish."

Three minutes later, in his office, Father Carmody put through a call to the Knight brothers.

20

Phil answered it.

"Have you heard?" a voice asked without preamble.

"Tell me."

"A body has been found in the lake. A young woman. A member of the faculty."

"What happened?" Phil had by now recognized the voice as Father Carmody's. Undeniably, he felt a lilt of excitement within, smoke in the nostrils of a fire horse too long inactive.

"We would all feel more comfortable if we knew you were close to the investigation."

"Representing the university?"

"Sub rosa."

Philip glanced at Roger, who was on the other phone.

"Secretly," whispered Roger, but he had forgotten to cover the receiver.

"Discreetly," added Father Carmody.

"Who is she?" Roger asked.

"Not someone I know. Amanda Pick."

"Amanda!" Roger cried.

"You knew her?"

"Where was she found?" Phil asked.

Philip listened to the priest's account and then agreed to meet him at the lakeside scene. He hung up and returned to his bowl of oatmeal. "Never work on an empty stomach." Roger, the only one within earshot of this sound advice, did not need it, although the call had apparently given him the same lift of excitement it had given Phil, with the added poignant factor that Roger had known the deceased.

"I'll come with you, of course."

There was no question that Roger would accompany Philip. Amanda! What a shock. Laura must already know. If she did not, informing her must fall to someone else. Roger would not have wanted the task of being the first to tell Laura Flynn that her housemate had been found dead in a campus lake.

The parka Roger put on had been inspired by those worn by the coaching staff. Roger pronounced it the most comfortable outer garment he had ever worn. Now, in his excitement, he needed help getting into it and Phil supplied it, anxious to get to Father Carmody. For some reason, Roger pulled the hood over his head as he lumbered out to the van.

"Why Father Carmody, Phil?"

"Why not?"

"One, he's retired. Two, he taught classics. He never worked in the Main Building."

But of course both brothers had heard that the new administration relied on Father Carmody as their link to the past. Once he had been an *éminence grise,* but now his hair was snow white. He had the simplicity and integrity at which the administrative mind marvels, stirred perhaps to memories of lost innocence. Seeking nothing, having nothing he was unwilling to lose, his was the power of the powerless. And Father Carmody was a man of great practical as well as theoretical wisdom. He had been instrumental in Roger's joining the Notre Dame faculty.

When Roger Knight had been offered the Huneker Chair of Catholic Studies at Notre Dame, he'd first felt a flush of excitement, but reflection had brought a more reasoned reaction. Although he had received his doctorate in philosophy from Princeton, he had been nineteen at the time, a Goodyear blimp of a boy, too insouciantly, if respectfully, dubious about received opinions to be employable. And too fat. After a tour in the navy, when his weight had melted from him in boot camp, only to reclaim its rightful place as he spent indolent hours in base libraries ingesting junk food and devouring books, he had settled down with his brother, Philip, a private investigator. Roger's fund of unusual knowledge, his prowess with the computer, had made him an asset to the firm, and the Knight brothers had prospered.

At the time the invitation from Notre Dame came, prompted by the huge success of Roger's book on Baron Corvo, the brothers were living in Rye, New York, having fled the terrors of the city to that redoubt of almost rural peace. Phil, thinking of sports, had been thrilled by the prospect of going to Notre Dame. The fraternal enthusiasm and the gentle importuning from South Bend decided Roger, and the brothers were soon ensconced at Notre Dame, where Roger roamed like a free variable over departmental divisions, able to offer any course that could be brought under the commodious title of Catholic Studies.

His main misgiving was one he had not anticipated: a shy sense of almost shame that he had achieved academic security at one fell blow, while young colleagues like Amanda Pick must pass through the anxious months of the tenure decision. Moreover, he had been prepared to feel a twinge of guilt for taking Phil from full involvement in his profession, but his older brother had found the campus endlessly interesting, with one sport or another offering almost daily diversion. From time to time Phil took a client, but he seemed to avoid cases that would demand the full exercise of his powers. Fearing that he had forced his brother into premature retirement, Roger repined. However unlucky for the victim, Phil was glad to be recalled to action when a body was found just offshore in Saint Joseph's Lake and Father Carmody asked him to represent the interests of the university.

"Which lake is Saint Joseph's, Roger?" Phil asked, as they came along the campus road.

"The one to the east. Why don't we just head for Holy Cross House?"

In the parking lot of Holy Cross House, entered from Douglas Road, several official vehicles were already parked. A red four-wheeler from the campus firehouse, with Brother Felix in the driver's seat, had been the first to arrive at the scene. He had quickly decided that help from the outside world was needed. By the time the paramedics got there, three squad cars from town had already joined the red four-wheeler. The paramedics were led down to where the body still lay half submerged in water.

Father Carmody was waiting for the Knight brothers in the parking lot and came forward to help extricate Roger from his swivel chair in the back of the van. The vehicle had been designed to accommodate Roger at his maximum weight; and since air travel was always problematic, given his girth, he and Phil had formed the habit of arriving at the site of a new case in the van. The dearth of new cases since Roger had joined the faculty at Notre Dame caused the little trip to Holy Cross House to revive pleasant memories of previous cases.

"It doesn't look as if they need me," Phil said, when they came around the building and looked down at the crowd of police and paramedics milling around the body, which had been taken from the water and now lay on the trampled snow.

Father Carmody took his arm. "I want you there to monitor everything and keep me informed."

Phil recognized Roy Gross in the group on the shore and moved ahead of Father Carmody down the hill to the lake.

Roy Gross was a tall, meatless man with a prominent nose and eyes that seemed to be looking for the lenses of his glasses rather than through them. He grunted when Phil came to a stop beside him and looked down at the lifeless body of the young woman the paramedics had removed from the water.

"Foul play?"

"She was found face down in the water, but how she died is unclear."

Clarity would come when the medical examiner arrived. The paramedics—the female with a crew cut, the male with a luxuriant ponytail—had sought to revive the woman but unsuccessfully.

"Water in her lungs?"

A shake of the head.

"So she didn't drown."

"I didn't say that." Caution brimmed in the ponytail's eyes, which then went up the hill to where the ME's vehicle had come into view.

Father Carmody went down to join Phil but Roger remained above, looking out at the lake like a ship in dry dock longing for the wash of waves against his side. "Beautiful!" Roger sighed.

He referred to the snow that had continued its immaculate slow descent during the grim proceedings by the lakeshore. The waters of the lake were dark and metallic, stirred by the slight breeze that brought snow in at an angle. The temperature was not much below freezing and on the rise so that the snow was damp and heavy, melting for the most part as soon as it landed on the path; but the grass was more hospitable. Ducks and geese, impervious to the change of weather, went about their incessant quest for food. It had still not struck Roger that the object lying down there on the shore of the lake was the mortal remains of Amanda Pick.

21

covery of the body, the sounding of the alarm, and the arrival of officialdom that Father Rush watched a large man come slipping and sliding along the pathway from the direction of the boathouse and heating plant.

His topcoat was open as well as his tweed jacket, exposing to the weather the shirted expanse of his considerable belly. His arms were akimbo, like stabilizing fins, and while his wild eyes looked ahead to what was going on at the place where the body had been found, his mind seemed to be on his feet and the glazed pathway. When he noticed the man approaching, Father Carmody went to intercept him. "Professor Pottery, you shouldn't be out in shoes like those."

"Is it true? Is it Amanda?"

Father Carmody murmured some of those consoling non sequiturs the clergy have available for such situations. At the same time, he turned toward Roger and beckoned him to come over. Roger's descent from the post he had taken on the snowy hill before Holy Cross House sufficiently distracted the newcomer. It would have been difficult to say whether Roger was walking, skiing, sliding, losing his balance, or practicing an intricate gavotte meant to be performed on a precipitous surface. But it was upright and puffing that he arrived at Father Carmody's side.

"Roger, you know Sean Pottery. He was a friend and colleague of the deceased."

"Deceased!" Pottery cried, struck by the finality of the word.

Roger took Pottery's hand and began to shake it vigorously. This formal gesture seemed oddly appropriate and Pottery calmed down. There was reason to think that Pottery should think Roger was privy to his doomed love for Amanda. How well-suited Pottery seemed for the role of rejected suitor.

"How was she killed?" Pottery asked.

"Killed? She drowned," Father Carmody said.

Pottery peered at Carmody as if he were toying with him. "Nonsense," he said.

"I don't think a cause of death has been determined," Roger put in.

Father Carmody drifted back to the investigation.

"They will say suicide, but it won't matter. They will have killed her," Pottery continued.

"They," it emerged, were the members of the Appointments and Promotion Committee of the philosophy department.

"You're in English, I believe."

"I knew the young woman."

"So did I."

This had no effect on Pottery.

"I have sat in on your courses," Roger said.

"I never understood what department you're in."

"I'm not in a department. My title is the Huneker Professor of Catholic Studies."

"Dear God." There was the smell of scotch when Pottery spoke.

On another occasion Roger would have laughed, if only to show that he did not take offense. But this was neither the time nor place. Pottery looked hesitantly toward the shore and the group to which Father Carmody had returned. Roger took Pottery's elbow and helped him ascend to the upper level. On any other occasion the sight of the gargantuan Roger giving assistance to the overweight and uncoordinated professor of English would have provoked mirth. But on this grim morning their climb went unnoticed except by the old man grinning on a bench. He lifted his hand, and Roger was about to return the greeting when he realized that they were being blessed. He steered Pottery toward the bench.

"Good morning, Father."

The old priest put a finger in his ear and gave it a twist. "I don't like to waste the battery. What did you say?"

"Can we share your bench?"

The old priest gave out a cry of pain. "Have you noticed the way people use the word 'share' nowadays? The other day our chaplain 'shared' a sermon with us. I told him I wanted the whole thing." The old priest widened his eyes and grinned.

"I am Roger Knight and this is Professor Pottery."

"Are you with the police?"

Pottery had been following the passage of the body bag from the lake up the hill to the parking lot, the burden being carried with some insouciance by people from the Medical Examiner's office. Now he seemed to collapse rather than sit down on the bench. He stared out over the lake, a man for whom the sun no longer shone, from whom gladness had been definitively stolen, to whom a terminal sorrow had come. Roger felt like Buridan's ass, who had died of indecision between two identical bales of hay; he was equally drawn to talk with the old priest and to ask Sean Pottery what he had meant by suggesting that the dead woman had been killed.

"Matthew Rush," the old priest said, as if he were answering a roll call. "How I missed this kind of weather during the years I was in Bangladesh."

"How long have you been back?"

"You never really leave, you know. It stays with you. The heat was horrible."

"Have you been sitting here long?"

"What's wrong with him?"

Pottery had begun to weep. His hands clasped his knees, he sat forward and wept open-eyed, his lower lip trembling, his

111

vast stomach rising and falling in the tide of grief. "I would have married her," Pottery sobbed. "I never knew if she understood that."

So it was that Roger found himself listening to simultaneous accounts of a mission parish in Bangladesh and the thwarted love of Sean Pottery for his junior colleague.

"I told her the tenure decision didn't matter. Not if we got married. But of course it mattered."

"Some years we baptized thousands. You probably wonder how much they understood of what they were doing, but how much do any of us understand? They are a wonderfully devout people. They put us to shame."

"I'm not much of a Catholic," Pottery said. "I was surprised to learn that she was quite devout."

"Old men spend hours on their knees. Silent prayer. They are natural mystics."

"I have made my living speaking, but I had no experience with such a thing. Oh, how I botched it."

"Huge families."

"She asked me once how so impractical a man as Chesterton could have such practical sense. That was one of her questions."

"A gift for abstract thought."

Pottery put his face in his hands and rocked back and forth on the bench.

"Carrying it down was harder than carrying it up," the old priest said, rising from the bench.

"I'd like to talk to you more, Father."

"I have been a priest for sixty-one years. Come to breakfast. Bring your friend."

Pottery had heaved himself to his feet, but he began to move across the now slushy lawn as if the disappearing body bag were a magnet and he steel filings.

Roger rose to his feet. "Perhaps we should seek shelter in Holy Cross House."

"You will be my guest," Father Rush said.

Pottery allowed himself to be led away by the ancient priest.

As Roger neared the building, Laura Flynn came toward him from the parking lot. "Roger!" she cried. "Roger."

22

in the role of buffer between the members of campus security
and the South Bend Police Force. This was an uneven contest
at best, since many campus cops had spent their active years as
members of the South Bend police. Those who had not were apt
to be men and women who had been forced to tailor their ambitions to the relatively undemanding tasks of a campus security
force. Some patrolled the campus on bicycles, wearing plastic
bubble hats that seemed to expose their cranium to the surgical
saw; others drove at fifteen to twenty mph cars designed for
speeds in the high seventies. Their revenge was to decorate the
windshields of faculty cars with citations on the pretense that
some regulation or another had been violated. Once campus
parking had been plentiful and random; now it was scarce and
so regulated that a professor was guaranteed a brisk walk from
his vehicle to his office. It was not true that a computer program
had been devised to discover the longest distance between A
(vehicle) and B (office). Even the pampered administration
complained, though most of them had a designated parking
place decorated with warnings worthy of Dante to anyone who
would presume to usurp it.

Roy Gross, once in homicide, now chief of campus security,
was particularly resented by the local constabulary in the matter
of the body in the lake. It wasn't what he said; it was his expression as he followed the proceedings with silent disapproval.

"Tell them for God's sake to stake out the scene," a city cop muttered to Phil. "I wonder exactly how much time went by before the Keystone Kops decided to call us?"

"Counting from when?"

And so the testy exchange might have continued but for the arrival of Earl Sanders. Earl and Roy had been partners. Earl was not so far from retirement that he could afford to alienate the chief of security at Notre Dame; he might want a job there in the near future. Besides, he had little confidence in Proudie, the coroner, a bookkeeper who had won office on a fluke and relied on his brother-in-law, an obstetrician, for medical advice. Fortunately, the medical examiner's staff was allowed to pursue its investigation without undue interference from Proudie.

The scene was photographed, examined, staked off, photographed some more, and a guard posted. The body had been taken away. Phil and Roy and Earl were given coffee in the refectory of Holy Cross House, the invitation conveyed by Roger, who had become the guest of Father Rush. A morose Pottery sat next to Father Rush and was staring into a coffee cup as into the depths of hell.

"Professor Pottery thinks that Amanda's death could be linked to the fact that she was coming up for tenure this year," Roger said.

"She would have gotten it!" Laura affirmed loyally.

"Tenure?"

The two policemen and Phil looked at Roger with incomprehension.

Phil's eyes traveled to Pottery, who was unaware of the attention he was receiving. Phil had an imperfect grasp of the concept of tenure. The first time Roger had explained it to him he was certain his brother was kidding. Absolute job security after six years on the faculty? A lifetime sinecure with few duties lived on this glorious campus, with multiple sports programs promising diversion throughout the year? It seemed too good to be true.

"It has some of the features of a medieval benefice," Roger had said, as if agreeing with an unvoiced thought of Phil's. "There have even been instances of pluralism."

He meant double-dipping, a man holding a professorship in two institutions, often at some distance from one another. What shocked Phil was the fact that the man had been able to acquit himself adequately in both institutions.

"That may explain the indignation."

But what Philip had yet to grasp was the intensity of the competition for tenured positions and the anguish suffered by the candidate during the period that a decision was being made.

"Tell me about it," Phil said, sitting next to Pottery. Laura had gone to console Blanche.

"They killed her," Pottery said fervently, and his three listeners nodded encouragement. What did the professor mean?

23

taken to a chair behind the counter of the nurses' station in
Holy Cross House. She had fled to the Loftus Center when she
escaped the horror and found her friend, Emily House. Emily
refused to jog and had given up walking as well. It was her custom, after putting in twenty minutes on a NordicTrack in Loftus
Center, to meet Blanche so that the two could breakfast
together at the North Dinng Hall. Describing for Emily the horror she had seen was not easy.

"Stop shrieking and tell me what you saw."

"A body!" Blanche cried, and her voice rose out of control.
"A woman's body, lying in the lake!"

It was not simply that Emily was morbid; she did not like
the thought of her friend rather than herself making such a discovery. She almost regretted her decision to stop accompanying
Blanche as she labored along the lake path. Once she understood what Blanche had found, it was imperative that Blanche
take her to the body so that she could claim to be codiscoverer.
Later, since Blanche, sitting in her chair behind the counter of
the nurses' station, was still in semishock, Emily talked to the
press in the person of Roland Kaylor from WNDU. Roland took
her outside, placed her under an elm tree, and directed questions at her, while a delinquent with a shoulder-mounted camera taped the interview.

"How did you come upon the body?"

There are moments when one's character is revealed, rein-
forced, or weakened, moments that are the moral crossroads of

life. One path is the path of righteousness and truth, the other that of mendacity and perdition. At Emily's age the bent twig had confirmed with growth its early divergence from the straight and true. The Emily that might have been would have corrected the question and given Blanche full credit. The Emily that was rolled her eyes and sighed. "It was the most harrowing experience of my life."

What she described was what she had seen when she made Blanche lead her reluctantly back along the lakeshore path. "I knew at once that it was Amanda."

Roland grew excited. This was the first identification of the body. "Who is she?"

Taken metaphysically, the question is unanswerable, but we approximate an answer by accumulating the contingencies that make up a human life. Who was Amanda Pick? Emily still worked part time in Human Resources, where she was affectionately known as "Old Hard Drive." She seemed to have embedded in her memory information about everyone ever employed at Notre Dame. It was simply a matter of calling up the Amanda Pick dossier. Alas, Emily's mind was not what it had been, and it was another but related personal record she called up on the screen of memory, that of Laura Flynn, a pardonable error, no doubt, since the two women had shared a house. No matter, when she realized her mistake, she was able to segue easily to Amanda. The information Emily had gathered—her sources were many—included members of the faculty, departmental secretaries, watchful women working in copying centers, the library check-out desk, and the University Club. It was from this cornucopia of secondhand information that Emily plucked the few nuggets she tossed to the reporter. Of course Emily selected only highlights of Laura's background, which, more accurately stated, say by the Recording Angel, would have gone something like this:

Laura Flynn, an economist, was in her seventh year on the faculty, but she had taught for several years on a lesser campus of the University of Minnesota. She had been persuaded to put herself forward for promotion to associate professor, a tenured position, encouraged by Corcoran, a member of the relevant committee. She had succumbed. But a worm of doubt had been introduced by the lifted brows and expressions of surprise by several female faculty members. What was Luke Corcoran up to?

The real or imagined doubts did little to bolster her self-esteem. This was not the compensating success she had longed for. Laura's marriage had not only disintegrated; her husband had managed to have it annulled, leaving her feeling like a nonperson. Understandably enough, she generalized from her own experience to the vulnerability of women in general. She, along with Bridget Quirk, another victim, was active in WOUND, Women of the University of Notre Dame. When Sean Pottery, a senior professor in the English department, got a crush on Laura's housemate, Amanda Pick, dropping in at all hours drunk, and Amanda refused to see how demeaning a relationship it was, Laura's feminist hackles were raised. Not that Amanda encouraged Pottery's advances, but she refused to take the necessary steps to put a definitive end to them. Amanda seemed unaware of the protections now available to women, even at Notre Dame. Sexual harassment was now recognized for what it was. Laura submitted a formal report to Jewel Fondue, the relevant local authority, and induced Amanda to sign it. But Laura wanted justice now.

Her chance came when Sean Pottery showed up drunk and Amanda was not home. Laura opened the door wide and let him in. "Come into my parlor," she said, making a little curtsy.

Pottery sat on the couch and Laura brought him a drink, bourbon and sweet vermouth, but in a tumbler. She had made her own Coke look like a similar drink. She sat next to him on the couch and lifted her glass in a toast. Pottery drank distractedly.

121

"I have to see her."

"She'll be here."

"I have to tell her something."

"Tell me."

She'd had to repeat it and he looked at her with eyes that didn't quite focus. She leaned toward him and smiled fetchingly, willing him to do something. Amanda had described the way he had lunged at her; Laura had witnessed it once. How long had it been since she had sat like this with a man? She told herself that what she was doing was entrapping him, getting him to act with her as he had with Amanda, and then she would sound the alarm. She moved closer to him, anticipating his arms around her. His lips were wet and his breath was heavy with the smell of drink. He didn't seem at all menacing. There was something sad about him, vulnerable. She put her hand on his and he looked down at it. His eyes seemed focused when he looked at her. She smiled up at him and lifted her face. Her eyes dropped to his mouth. She seemed drawn to his lips as bees are drawn to nectar, but before their lips could meet he leapt to his feet with a roar, pushing her away from him as he did so.

She sprawled on the floor and he stood over her, looking down at her with contempt. "I intend to file a complaint about this!"

Then Pottery reeled toward the door, pulled it open, and disappeared.

Such truths were unknown to Emily, but she did the best with what she had heard.

"She had brought a charge of sexual harassment against a senior professor in another department," Emily said, and the reporter's eyes widened.

"Whom did she accuse?"

"Sean Pottery. I don't know that this is public knowledge."

"Tell me about him."

"That's him over there. The fat man."

"There are two fat men."

"The one facing us."

"Those must be police with him," Roland said.

"I suppose they've arrested him."

Roland was drawn across the room as cartoon mice are drawn by the scent of cheese. Emily was relieved to have him go. As long as she was talking with him, the opportunity to correct her account was there. Now she felt almost absolved from her treachery. It was no longer in her hands.

When Roger met Laura outside the building, he gathered her into his arms and held her, at once dreading and hoping for an outburst of tears. But after a moment Laura looked up at him. Her eyes were damp but she was under control. "Roger, what happened?"

"Come."

He led her inside but not to the table where Pottery was in the custody of the old missionary, Father Rush, who was smiling benevolently as if he was personally responsible for this unwonted commotion at breakfast in Holy Cross House. The tenor of the day there was not often varied, and one had to rely on memories of one's active life for diversion. The staff was competent and caring but inevitably adopted the tone of parent to child when addressing the old priests, often employing the vacuous first person plural. "Did we have a bowel movement?" "How did we sleep last night?" Somehow such questions became impersonal, but the line between the public and private was blurred beyond recall.

"When did you last see Amanda?" Roger asked Laura.

"I checked her room just now when I got the call. I had no idea she wasn't there."

"You thought she was home last night?"

Laura nodded, her eyes filled with remembered horror. What a shock it must have been to be told that someone she thought was sleeping in the house had just been found dead in a campus lake.

"She must have gotten up early to jog," Roger said.

"Jog? Amanda didn't jog. Apparently she had no need of exercise."

Roger's expression did not alter. "She was found on the jogging path. In jogging clothes."

Laura reacted to this with incredulity.

"When exactly did you last see her, Laura?"

"I went to bed early. About nine. Maybe later."

She did not, of course, realize that these were questions she would be asked again and again. Last night Laura was weary from the long day, but Amanda was on edge, knowing that the time until her tenure decision was made was growing shorter.

"There were just the two of you in the house?"

"Yes. She was on the phone when I went to bed. She was desperate for any information about the tenure decision."

"Whom did she call? The chair?"

"Oh, he wouldn't have told her."

All the proceedings of a tenure decision were confidential, and members of the committee were bound to silence. In practice this meant that they told others in confidence, trusting that their interlocutor would be made of sterner moral stuff than themselves.

"What did Amanda herself think of her prospects?"

"She vacillated between thinking she had no chance and that she would make it. Yesterday she was down. It all seems so unimportant now, doesn't it?"

It seemed clear that those tenure proceedings would assume great importance in the effort to discover what had happened to Amanda Pick.

"Isn't that Sean Pottery?" Laura had leaned forward and whispered her question, tipping her head toward the table across the room.

"Pottery has gone into full mourning."

Laura raised her brows. "If he had any gossip about how things were going, he would have told Amanda everything."

"Would she have called him?"

"You know he had a kind of crush on Amanda."

"She told me something of that. You don't think she would have telephoned him?

Laura thought about it. "Last night she might have. She had to know."

"He seems heartbroken."

"Does he?"

"You sound dubious."

"It's just that I know how he pestered Amanda." Laura's voice dropped, and while she continued to look at Roger her thoughts were not on him. After a moment she shuddered and her eyes came back into focus.

"I can't believe she is really dead."

Roger reached out a hand to put on hers. For a moment, he thought that Laura would snatch hers away, but then she let her little hand be covered by his.

Roger continued to seek clarity in the welter of detail. Pottery, when he was keening on the bench outside, had given no indication that he might have talked with Amanda the night before. Perhaps he had. Perhaps he had been with her. The theatrical grief of the professor was excessive enough to be suspicious— at least to the suspicious—and there were those here whose function it was to suspect. Roger asked Laura to refresh his mind as to Amanda and Pottery's relationship.

"He was crazy about her. He made a pest of himself."

"His affection was not returned?"

"Look at him."

"His weight?"

She put her free hand over his, her face an apologetic

mask. "That isn't what I meant, Roger. You know it isn't. He's pathetic."

"A man in love can be a comic sight."

"He just wouldn't leave her alone. I urged her to lodge a complaint."

"A complaint."

"There is a campus harassment office."

"It was that bad?"

"They couldn't actually do anything to him unless Amanda was willing to follow up on her complaint, which she wasn't. She regretted even lodging it. Perhaps she thought it lent more importance to Sean Pottery than he really had in her life."

"He would have known about the tenure decision?"

"He knows people on the committee."

Roger looked at her. "So she had alienated someone who could influence her academic destiny?"

"Oh, she had enemies enough in her own department."

"Tell me about that."

24

sustained by a vast infrastructure of grievances, not least among them the size of the office assigned her on the eleventh floor of Grace, a former residence hall that had been remodeled and turned to administrative use when its perpendicular isolation had proved to thwart the purposes of campus residence life. At most, residents had seen one another in the elevators, perhaps in the diminutive chapel hidden behind a first-floor common room designed as what was called, at the time, a conversation pit. Grace had been like a hotel whose fugitive guests were unknown to one another. Remodeled to the tune of millions, it now provided similarly inhuman circumstances for various business offices—publications, publicity, alumni, accounting. The Office of the Counselor for Student Complaints, with particular emphasis on unwonted sexual advances, was a small, square room with a single window that gave a view of a parking lot, the geodesic dome of Stepan Center, and a corner of the new Warren Golf Course. At that window Jewel Fondue spent much of her day brooding in what she thought of as her Rumplestiltskin mood.

It was difficult now to recall the triumph that had been hers the day the trustees had been persuaded, against their bent and with little support from the administration, to fund an office that would handle complaints of sexual harassment.

"Are there any?" Jewel had been asked at the crucial meeting.

"That's the point."

"How do you mean?"

"Where would a young woman lodge a complaint?"

"You think there would be complaints if there were an office to receive them?"

Jewel had smiled knowingly at Melanie Combes, a female CEO of a company she had inherited from her parents.

P. J. Wilcox, who prefaced every remark with the statement that he had five daughters, wondered if encouraging such complaints was in the interest of the university.

"I am thinking of the young women," Jewel said primly.

"What young women?"

"Those subject to sexual harassment."

"But are there any?"

Jewel came dangerously close to promising a dozen complaints the first semester. But she had remained patient, the resolution had been passed, and she had been named, after considerable further debate about her title, Counselor for Student Complaints. The victory celebration had been held in the lounge of Grace Hall, sponsored by Gender Studies, the program in which Jewel had taught prior to her presumed elevation to the post she had been advised not to call the CSC.

She had moved into her office in July and for months she had felt like the Maytag repair man, sitting at her window staring out at the triangular elements of Stepan's geodesic dome and actually missing Gender Studies. She was teaching a single course this fall, her swan song, "Didos, Dodos, and Dildoes," but half the students were male athletes who were twice as wide as the chairs they sat in. Enemies claimed that grade inflation had been the key to keeping the program going, but the charge assumed that the program was flourishing. Jewel had been relieved to retreat to her sinecure on the eleventh floor of Grace. At first. But there is nothing more enervating than inactivity.

In September a sophomore with slightly crossed eyes and pursed lips found her way to Jewel's door. A religious woman

128

would have intoned a Te Deum, but Jewel's elation was short-lived. The object of the student's complain was a female assistant dean. Jewel convinced the girl that she had misunderstood the situation. Later she left a stern voice message for the assistant dean. Don't let down the side. Her own phone was clogged with messages from mean-spirited conservatives who sought her advice on depilatories, karate, and the best techniques for sexual advancement. Not until Amanda Pick did the clouds lift and the sun shine through.

"Tell me exactly what happened."

"I'm only here as a favor to Laura Flynn."

"One has need of friends at times like these."

"Laura makes too much of it."

"Of what?"

"It's so silly. Laura isn't suspicious of Fred Cossette."

"Who is he?"

"A graduate student."

Jewel sighed away this irrelevancy.

"Amanda, I can't help you if I don't know."

"I'm not sure you can anyway. He's a senior member of the faculty, but he isn't in my department. Laura thinks that because he knows the people on the philosophy A&P Committee . . . " She let the thought complete itself.

"Laura thinks he will influence the decision as to your tenure?"

"He's in English. He has no influence in my department."

"You mean direct influence?"

"I mean influence. Look, I told you, these are Laura's suspicions, not mine."

"But Pottery has been on the faculty forever. He knows the old guard in your department, doesn't he?"

"Of course he knows them, but that doesn't mean . . . "

Jewel smiled grimly. It seemed to be a classic case. The man wraps himself in the authority of his role and does not have to say explicitly that he will see that tenure is denied unless . . .

"What exactly has he done?"

"He wants me to marry him."

"Marry him!"

"He sent me a letter. Handwritten. He has a beautiful cursive style."

Amanda was a lovely young woman in her early thirties, with raven-colored hair, green eyes, and a mouth that pouted sensuously when she wasn't smiling. Her smile revealed large, sparkling teeth. Her olive-green dress with a full skirt was enlivened by the colorful shawl she wore. It had slipped down onto her arms, and although little but her face and hands were visible, she somehow gave the impression of peeping in the buff around some tree in the Garden of Eden. Of course she was attractive to men. But how was a marriage proposal to be construed as sexual harassment? Jewel put the question to Amanda and her confused hesitation said it all. They stared at one another across Jewel's desk.

"Would you like coffee, Amanda?"

"I prefer tea."

She had to go down the hall for water, but Jewel took the trouble and made tea for Amanda. Over the course of the next half hour, Jewel came to believe that an offer of marriage from a man with friends on Amanda's tenure committee was not without its menacing overtones.

"What did he do when you refused?"

"Oh, I haven't refused."

"You were afraid to?"

"I don't know what to do."

Jewel made her another cup of tea. This would take time but the situation had promise. Besides, Jewel's calendar was clear and she had all morning. Eventually she turned to her computer and composed a memo, summarizing what Amanda had told her.

"Sign that," she said, when she had printed it out.

Amanda read the statement and began to shake her head as she did so. "It sounds so silly."

"Not to me."

"The reason I haven't said yes . . ."

"Yes?"

"There is someone else."

"He has another woman!" The image of a monster formed in Jewel's mind.

"No, no. I do."

But all Jewel could get out of Amanda was a name, Noah Beispiel, and then Amanda left.

Perhaps priests felt like this, made privy in their confessionals to another's secrets, and then, poof, the penitent is gone. Amanda did not return. She did not take Jewel's calls. But it was not in Jewel's nature to accept defeat—after all, she had refused to be defeated by her gender. But it was in vain that she tried to interest the administration in opening an inquiry into the matter. She met with enigmatic incomprehension in the form of Father Finn, but finally wrested from the man permission to speak to the university counsel. Here Jewel met a stone wall in the guise of a willowy woman in a tailored suit, whose ample proportions seemed sacrificed on the altar of her vocational ambitions. And she had clearly cast off any sense of solidarity with her sex. In vain did Jewel seek to get through to the woman, girl to girl, so to speak, powder room confiding.

"Let me put it this way, Jewel, what if this woman should bring a suit against the university?"

"I wish she would."

"Perhaps your wish will be granted. If it is, you can see that I would be in a rather odd situation if I had earlier seemed to prejudge the case in her favor and against my eventual client in such a possible suit."

It was the actual suit the woman wore, padded shoulders, pin stripes, that told Jewel her cause was lost in this office. Even so, she did not admit defeat. She chose to beard the lion in his den. One evening she sat down at Professor Pottery's table in the bar of the Morris Inn.

"Good afternoon, Professor."

"This table is taken."

"This chair was not."

He trained a bloodshot eye on her. "Who are you?"

"It is *what* I am that should give you concern."

"Indeed."

"I am the Counselor for Student Complaints."

"There is no such office. There cannot be."

"I am not surprised that you should wish there weren't."

"I expressed no wish."

"We come to the help of women who have been sexually harassed."

"What does that mean?"

Jewel leaned toward him, momentarily sickened by the fumes rising from the ashtray on the table. Pottery's lips were moist with drink, and his eyes were bright with malice. Jewel's plan had been to proceed by indirection, to hint, imply, sow fear in the man without really saying or threatening anything. But his smug complacency as he sat there, wreathed in tobacco smoke and reeking with drink, overcame her resolution.

"I'll tell you what it *could* mean. It could mean a senior professor making a nuisance of himself with a junior member of the philosophy department. It could mean that professor showing up drunk at that young professor's house and making unseemly advances and being taken away by the police. It could mean . . ."

She was stopped by the drink he dashed in her face. She rose to her feet, sputtering, liquor running down her face. Her beautiful silk blouse was soaked with alcohol. A hand closed around her arm and she turned to see the uniformed bartender.

"Did you see what he just did?"

"Come on, lady. Let's go. You can't act up like that in here."

"That's my drink all over her." Pottery's voice was shrill with indignation.

"Because you threw it at me!"

Pottery put back his head and laughed scornfully. "Raoul," he said to the bartender, whose hand was painfully tight on Jewel's upper arm. "Have you ever known me to throw away a drink in my life?"

Jewel was actually hustled from the bar. Early diners were clustered outside, waiting to be taken to their tables. Several people noticed the condition of Jewel's clothing. She fled through the lobby and to her car, where she sat behind the wheel and sobbed helplessly. She had said and written much about injustice, she had lamented long and loud the treatment of women by men, but never, never in her life had she been subjected to such abuse, and then . . .

She shut her eyes against the memory. Sean Pottery had triumphed over her. She had been thrown out of the Morris Inn bar! How many witnesses would there be. Of course they would all collude against her and endorse the absurd suggestion that she had taken Pottery's drink and spilled it all over herself. Oh, how she hated him! She beat her fists against the steering wheel of her car and wailed aloud.

That had seemed to be the end of the Amanda Pick complaint against Prof. Sean Pottery. The memo of her visit was stored on Jewel's computer, the sole result of nearly a semester on the job, not counting voice mail.

When Jewel heard that Amanda's body had been found offshore at one of the campus lakes, she had no doubt in the world what had happened or who was responsible. She picked up her phone and called the university counsel.

25

bearded Harvey Michaels sat before his computer, eyes closed, fingers poised over the keyboard like a concert pianist awaiting the fall of the baton, mentally constructing his topic sentence. And then his fingers dropped to the keys.

"The body of Dr. Amanda Pick, assistant professor of government, was found this morning by Saint Mary's Professor Emerita Blanche Crowley as she jogged around Saint Joseph's Lake."

He paused, read what he had written, and found it good. Public relations writing is a species of fiction. Art is the perfection of the thing made. He could hear Joe Evans repeat this Thomistic definition in a classroom of yesteryear. But then came doubt. Would Mort Maine, his pedantic boss, suggest that "she" was of ambiguous reference? The image of a corpse moving along the jogging path danced before his eyes like an errant cursor. But a complete avoidance of ambiguity was impossible in this Valley of Tears. He left the sentence as it was. When his phone rang, his mind was still on what he was writing.

"This is Fred Cossette. I want to make a statement about the death of Amanda Pick."

Harvey pushed away from his computer, and his wheeled desk chair gathered momentum as it headed for the wall. When it struck, Harvey's head snapped forward. Whiplash in his own workplace?

"What kind of a statement?"

"I don't want to make it on the phone."

Harvey's mind was racing. When he was young he had dreamt of becoming a newsman, his name a household word, an Eric Severeid or Walter Cronkite, a man adept in many media, a commentator who wrote his own stuff and was often sent on dangerous assignments to hitherto unknown trouble spots on the globe. After graduation from Notre Dame, he had written copy for a Chicago PR firm for a time, then snatched at the opportunity to return to his alma mater. In moments of self-knowledge he realized that his was a diminished life, almost indolent, riddled with routine. The death of Amanda Pick had come almost as a welcome relief, but this telephone call was like receiving the governor's reprieve.

"Where are you?"

"In the Huddle."

Harvey thought about that. He liked it. He could be at the campus eatery in minutes, and chances were that it was crowded and he could talk to this caller unobserved.

"How will I know you?" He tried a Jason Robards's expression; he squinted like Robert Redford. If only there were an underground garage on campus in which to meet, but the water table made that unfeasible. It seemed easier to tell Fred Cossette how he could recognize Harvey Michaels.

"A beard?"

"Going gray," Harvey added. It seemed the guarantee of maturity and experience.

When Harvey entered the Huddle and looked around the large room and the several hundred students lined up at the different counters, depending on whether they wanted Italian, stir-fry, hamburgers, or Mexican, he knew a moment of doubt. The call had been a hoax; he was suddenly sure of it. He replayed the voice in his memory, trying to identify it. It seemed clearly disguised. A hand touched his shoulder. "You Michaels?"

Fred Cossette was holding a tray on which were four tacos and two containers of Coke. What was the ethical judgment on being fed, literally, by a source? Harvey had never refused a taco in his life. They went to a table in the middle of the room and Harvey sat across from the man. And he was a man, not a student. It turned out he was a graduate student in government.

"Amanda Pick was in philosophy. Was"—he shook his head at the past tense—"I was dating her housemate."

Harvey was into his first taco, but his eyes remained on Fred. "Why did you call me?"

"Because this is a legal matter."

Harvey fell silent. Switch the last two digits of his number and you got the university counsel. Did Fred think he was a lawyer? Harvey finished the taco and sat back.

"The number you called was publicity."

Cossette looked at him expressionlessly. If he laughed, Harvey was going to throw the Coke at him. After a moment, Cossette began to nod his head. "Maybe that's all right."

"How so?"

"A *felix culpa*." When Harvey did not react, he added, "That's what Saint Augustine called Original Sin, 'a happy fault.' "

"What happened to Amanda Pick?"

"I'll give you a name."

"I already have a name."

"Sean Pottery. He is a full professor."

"What about him?"

"He was in love with Amanda."

"Whose housemate you were dating?"

"Well, we've gone out a couple of times. We get along."

"What about Professor Pottery?" Harvey had always been impervious to Pottery's appeal. He listened to Cossette's story of Pottery's drunken visits to Amanda's house and of his hostility to her when sober. "He also knew the senior members on the committee that was deciding whether or not she would get tenure."

Maybe a reporter would have been interested in this, the

137

reporter Harvey had imagined himself to be on the way to the Huddle. But a flack who wrote publicity for the university had no use for this kind of information.

"You'd better get in touch with the police."

"Shouldn't I talk to the university counsel?"

"She'd tell you to call the police."

"She?"

"It's a long story."

It was with a slow step that Harvey returned to his computer and the bland official statement of Amanda Pick's death. "Do not ask for whom the bell tolls." It's usually a wrong number.

A voice message awaited him from Jewel Fondue. He had to look the name up in the campus phone book to find out who she was. She answered on the first ring. "Counselor for Student Complaints."

"This is Harvey Michaels. You called?"

"There's something the university counsel should know."

Harvey lapsed into monosyllabic Anglo-Saxon. "This is publicity."

Silence. "I called the university counsel."

"You missed."

thought of themselves as the noonday devils when they arrived at the University Club for their regular Tuesday lunch. That was because they came at eleven-thirty to be fussed over by Karen the manager and Debbie the hostess and to get started on the executive martinis that made retirement tolerable.

"A body was found in the lake this morning," Debbie said.

"A body of water?"

"The human body is 90 percent water."

"More."

"A woman."

"Dead?"

"Dead."

The unoiled creak of time's chariot was not wholly unwelcome. Plato said philosophizing is learning how to die. In the end, we are all philosophers—if we're lucky.

"Who was she?"

"She was on the faculty."

This was news indeed. But like so much of what went on now, it reminded Bird and Leader of past events.

"Remember the tramp who was found dead in an air duct of the Main Building?"

"There was the cleaning woman murdered in Aerospace."

"Where else?"

The lawyers at their table were discussing the body in the lake. None of them had known the woman alive.

"A rapist?" asked a little lawyer, hunching forward, her features hamsterlike.

"Why would you say that?"

"She was murdered."

"You asked about rape."

"A woman jogging around the lake at the crack of dawn . . ."

"It was a jogger who found her."

"Another woman."

"Wasn't there ice on the lake."

"Not yet."

"Imagine if the lake had frozen over . . ."

"If it's rape, the coroner will find out."

"Let's hope so."

The hamster squinted, unsure whether she was being twitted.

"Where the hell is Security when you need them?" Coach Kelly inquired at the jock table.

"Who needs them?" Ray Brach wanted to know.

Hank Frailey shook his head. "The campus isn't safe anymore."

"It never was." Father Riehle removed his cigar to say this, then restored it to his clenched teeth.

At various tables in the University Club, over sandwiches in the Decio lunchroom, at the Morris Inn, and almost everywhere else on campus, the subject of the day was the death of Amanda Pick.

27

ally performed on the body of Amanda Pick confirmed the suspicion that her death had not been due to drowning. In all likelihood she had been dead when she was thrown into the lake.

"Thrown?" Philip Knight asked.

Roy Gross thought about it. "Placed."

"So she died on dry land? What was the cause?"

"Asphyxiation."

"Strangled?"

"Well, the bump on the head didn't kill her, but there are no marks on the throat."

There are many ways of stopping a person from breathing, some of them surprisingly easy to accomplish. A pillow held firmly over the face, for example. Had she met her death there by the lake, on the path along which Blanche Crowley had come jogging? Militating against this was the fact that she had been dead for at least two hours when she was found. Maybe three.

"So it happened this morning."

"She was found about seven."

"How long had she been in the water?"

Proudie tugged at his earlobe; Phil half expected the coroner's eyes to respond to the tugging, but they were trained on his notebook. The tip of his tongue appeared. "Not as long as she was dead."

"So her dead body must have been brought to the lake."

"It looks like it."

Phil asked Roy, "Where are you going to start?"

"I am told that the Counselor for Student Complaints wants to talk to me."

Phil wished Gross well and they parted at the war memorial the students called Stonehenge. He felt slightly duplicitous for not telling Roy and Harvey that Father Carmody had asked him to represent the university in the matter of Amanda's death. Not that he would keep anything from the police—after talking with Father Carmody. Meanwhile he wanted to talk with Amanda's housemate, Laura.

"You're Roger's brother."

"His big brother. Older brother." Phil was in excellent physical shape, not a spare pound on him. Once, briefly, Roger had been similarly thin. But Phil did not believe that his own frame could support the kind of weight Roger bore. Clearly being Roger's brother was all the recommendation he needed with Laura. She asked him in and offered him hot chocolate.

"With marshmallows?"

"Of course. You really are his brother."

"Did you have any idea this might happen to Amanda?"

Laura sighed. "I can't tell you how many times I have been asked that question since it happened. I actually made a statement to the police; I mean, they wrote it down."

"I won't write down what you say."

Laura smiled forlornly and gave him what was now a pretty practiced account of things. Of course she had already talked to Roger, so Phil would compare his impressions with his brother's.

By the time he did that, later that night, he knew a good deal more, and thinking it over, he didn't like it. Given the pressure of being up for tenure, in the phrase, and convinced that she would not get it, it was difficult not to think of suicide; but the medical examiner had definitely ruled out that possibility. Amanda had been suffocated, perhaps on the lake path, perhaps not, and then put into the water, as if to create the impression of a drowning. But she had not drowned. It was possible that she had been killed elsewhere and the dead body brought to the lake. There were, accordingly, unanswered questions about the exact way she had been killed and even where it had happened. But these were questions best left to the police laboratory. The more important question was who killed Amanda.

Initial indications pointed to Professor Pottery. He had been seen leaving the parking spot in front of his town house at a very early hour. This had been noticed because the professor was a notoriously late riser. It was said that he had not had a morning class in more than a dozen years. Asked about his early departure, he had replied that there were things he wanted to do in his campus office.

"That is why I received the news there." He had looked around at his inquirers. "I cannot meet my class this afternoon."

This had been registered without comment. What comment could he have expected from Gross and Harvey?

"I shall go into mourning. I will wear black like Belloc for the rest of my life."

The police had been told that Professor Pottery was something of a nut so they took this in stride. He was asked if it was true that he had a romantic interest in the deceased.

"A romantic interest," he had repeated incredulously. "So you really do talk that way."

His version of his passion for Amanda had emerged as a kind of aria. He had not understood his feelings at first; he had fought against them when it was already far too late. Only when fortified by drink had he found the courage to bare his heart to her.

"What was her reaction?"

"She was as surprised as I had been."

Sober he had recalled fragments of what he had done while drunk and been ashamed. This had led him to pretend disdain and dislike for the woman he loved. "But that was a ruse. Finally I proposed that we marry."

"What did she say?"

143

"I was still awaiting her response. I made the proposal in a letter, to give her more time to ponder it."

"You were optimistic?"

"No! I am unworthy of her. But I hoped against hope."

Pottery was a potpourri of attitudes, stances, mannerisms: His life seemed an impromptu drama in which, of course, he starred. It was difficult to take him seriously as a lover, let alone one who might be so enraged by rejection as to kill the one he loved. He seemed to anticipate the objection and addressed it with an imperfectly remembered stanza of Wilde's.

> *Now each man kills the one he loves.*
> *By each this must be heard*
> *The coward does it with a kiss*
> *The brave man with a sword.*

But the complaint Amanda had signed against Pottery, along with the circumstanced report Jewel Fondue had written on the case, gave a quite different picture of the relationship between Pottery and Amanda.

"It was absurd of him to think that she could like him in that way," Laura told Philip. "She admired him for his knowledge, especially of Chesterton, and he misunderstood. Fred Cossette is convinced that Pottery killed Amanda. The way she described him drunk he was capable of anything. The problem is he doesn't remember everything when he's sober."

Did Laura think Pottery had killed Amanda? She thought about it for some minutes.

"I want to say yes."

"But you won't?"

"The best I can do is maybe."

"You expressed surprise that Amanda was jogging that morning."

"Because she never had before."

It was the jogging that introduced a new twist to what had

happened to Amanda or, more precisely, the costume she wore.

"What does WOUND stand for?"

"What?"

Phil touched the fingers of his hands together before he realized it was a gesture he was copying from Roger. "I thought it was an acronym."

"It is. It stands for Women of the University of Notre Dame. Actually, it was an idea that fizzled. Bridget Quirk in philosophy and I are the only ones I know of who bought jackets."

"And Amanda?"

Laura shook her head. "No."

"But she was wearing a jacket with WOUND on the back."

This was the first Laura had heard of that, and she reacted with surprise. But then she understood. "She must have borrowed mine. Of course she did. She had nothing of her own to wear if she decided on the spur of the moment to go running. She wasn't a bit athletic."

The thought occurred to her at the same time it occurred to Phil. Had Amanda been mistaken for Laura? Had the wrong woman been killed that morning?

The possibility that Amanda had been killed by someone thinking she was Laura, misled by the legend on the hooded jogging jacket she wore, a legend to be found on only one other jacket, that of Bridget Quirk, took on plausibility with difficulty. With Bridget it would take more than a hood to cause anyone to think she was Amanda or Laura. The precision was necessary to respond to Roger's reasonable question. "But what if she were mistaken for Bridget?"

Roger did not contest the answer, but it was clear that he thought one jogging female looked pretty much like any other. Roger had had the thought to question Father Rush more

145

closely, and Phil had driven him back to Holy Cross House and sat over coffee in the refectory with Roger and the ancient priest, whose thoughts were always being pulled back to Bangladesh.

"Did you see a woman running on that path that morning, Father?"

"Yes."

"Are you sure?"

"I see her every morning."

"You do?"

"She goes around twice. The first time, she ran right past it, but the second time she was going much slower and then she saw it."

"The body in the lake?"

"That's what it turned out to be."

"What time is it when you take your bench out front?"

"I walk in the parking lot first."

"At what time?"

"Just before."

"I understand. What time do you get up in the morning?"

"In Bangladesh I always had to struggle to get out of bed in the morning. Not in this weather. Sometimes I don't think I am entirely asleep all night. Getting out of bed is no more difficult than going to bed."

"What time is it when you get out of bed?"

"Around five."

"Five in the morning!" Phil broke in.

"They won't let me say mass then; that's why I got in the habit of going outside."

Roger nodded. "And first you walk in the parking lot. How long?"

"How long is the parking lot?"

"No, how long do you walk? You get up at five. How much time elapses before you go outside?"

"None. I shave later. I like to say my prayers first."

"That's what you do while walking in the parking lot."

"They lock the sacristy. I check it every morning, and then I go outside."

"Shortly after five."

Father Rush agreed. "You make it sound like I'm on a schedule. I wish I were."

"How long do you pray in the parking lot?"

"I go up and down several times; then I go around front to sit on a bench. I say my rosary there."

"That's the way it was the morning they found the body?"

"I saw it first. I figured that lady jogger would notice it."

"I would say it was about fifteen minutes after five when you sat down on the bench. Does that sound right to you?"

"I've stopped wearing a watch."

"Just calculating."

"I guess so."

"And you have a pretty good view of the lake path."

He did. At first he thought praying outside was nothing but distraction—birds, squirrels, chipmunks, rabbits, all those ducks on the lake—but he had come to think differently.

"Benedicite omnia opera Domini Domino."

"Very apt," Roger said.

"What does it mean?" Phil asked.

" 'All ye works of the Lord bless the Lord.' It's from a psalm."

"I still say the breviary in Latin. I would say mass in Latin too if they would let me say my own."

Phil was wondering about the value of Roger's calculations. If Father Rush had taken up his post on the bench at 5:15 and the body was not discovered until 7:30 or so, the old guy would have had to be sitting out there in the morning chill for over two hours. But when Phil put it to the old priest, he saw no problem.

"After my prayers, I could sit there all day, just going over things. A man my age has many memories, and there aren't many survivors with the same memories to talk them over with.

147

Sometimes, I pick a definite year and go through it month by month. You'd be surprised how it comes back."

"It's too bad you weren't on watch early. The coroner places the death three or four hours before the body was found."

Father Rush nodded. "I didn't know it was a body."

"It would be something to establish that she died there."

"Oh, she was brought there."

"Brought there? How do you know that."

"I saw it. I watched the man carry something down those steps to the lake. When he came up again without it, I wondered what it was. That's when I saw something in the lake and sat there hoping that lady runner would notice it."

28

sibility that Amanda might have been killed on the mistaken impression that she was Laura. An odd sense of guilt swept over her, as if she should be lying dead and not Amanda, as if she had failed to fulfill some role meant for her. The obvious condition of that possibility did not immediately occur to her.

"Who would want to kill you?" Phil asked her.

"Oh, my God."

The obvious answer to that question was her former husband. Did Laura think he would seek to do her harm?

"He already has."

"I mean kill you?"

"It was Tony who did it! It has to be him."

Laura described his recent visit to campus and the lies he had told Amanda. Despite her certainty, it seemed unlikely that a man could mistake someone else for his own ex-wife, particularly when the person actually killed was someone he had spoken with.

Jewel Fondue was equally adamant when Phil talked with her. "She had been married. He's not her husband anymore, Laura was granted an annulment, but he still thinks he is."

Tony, the former husband, if that was the way to put it, lived in Minnesota, where he taught on one of the campuses of the state university.

"Laura came from there. Notre Dame was a great step up

for her, but it turned them into a commuting couple. With predictable results."

He asked her to explain that and she did. When graduate students marry they both intend to seek academic employment, and it is no easy matter to land positions in the same institution. More often than not, the husband taught in one college and the wife in another, sometimes hundreds if not thousands of miles apart. They would vow to meet regularly, sharing weekends in a mutually convenient town, meaning at an airport motel. Of course they would have Thanksgiving and Christmas together and the whole glorious summer. That was the plan. In the event, one or the other would begin to cancel weekend reunions because of the demands on his or her time. Months would go by with nothing to connect the spouses but the long-distance telephone. Loneliness created vulnerability; temptations occurred. An intolerable strain was put on such marriages, and frequently a couple collapsed under it.

"They escaped all that when they were both hired at Mankato, and then Laura was offered a job here."

"But not her husband."

"There was hope at first that an offer would be made to him, but it never materialized. They became a commuting couple. And then Laura heard that he was having an affair . . ."

Of course Phil had not known the deceased, but Laura's reaction to the news of her husband's infidelity had been so immediate it sounded as if she had been awaiting the change. She asked if he meant to divorce her. He said he would do better than that; he would have their marriage annulled. And he did.

"So as a Catholic she could have married again."

Jewel made a face. "Not again. The annulment means that she had never been married to him."

"How did Laura take it?"

If being unfaithful had put him at a disadvantage, the application for an annulment gave Tony the high ground. He was enlisting the church on his side.

"He ended up being the wronged party."

"Did they ever try to reconcile?"

"She offered to. Once. When he said no, it was as if a great imbalance had been corrected. Not that she accepted the annulment. She considered them still married and he knew it, and no court, civil or ecclesiastical, could change that."

"What about the woman he was going with?"

"Maybe he still is."

Phil gave up. Roger had become a Catholic and that meant it made sense, but Phil had to admit that there were times that he simply could not understand Roger's coreligionists. As a private investigator, he did not have to be told that marriages fell apart. When he had been establishing the firm, he had taken his share of divorce cases, but no more. There may be no-fault divorces in the legal sense, but he had never known a case in which one or both of the parties did not blame the other. However common it had become, divorce was still a wrenching experience for most people, an admission that a promise that had been meant to last a lifetime was being abrogated. How could one make that same promise to someone else and be certain to keep it? But annulment cut far deeper than that. Roger had Father Carmody explain it to Phil.

"There has to be free consent. If someone marches you down the aisle with a shotgun in your back, you can go through the marriage ceremony and say 'I do' out of fear, but it would be no marriage."

"That seems to be a pretty clear case."

Father Carmody frowned. "Some marriage courts accept claims of psychological inability to make such a promise that other courts would not."

Catholic divorce? The priest winced when Phil suggested this.

Obviously he thought that many annulments were given on questionable bases.

The phone rang and Phil rose to go, but Laura indicated that he should wait. She had turned away when she put the phone to her ear but almost immediately she turned and made a face. Her eyes rolled upward.

"I know, Jewel, I know. Of course they should be told."

While the logistical requirements of getting his brother, Roger, to Grace Hall, through the door and up the elevator to the Office of the Counselor for Student Complaints, were not impossible of realization, they represented the ordinary features of existence that were, because of his ponderous weight, extraordinary for Roger.

"Do you mean he's handicapped?" Jewel asked on the phone, the tone of her voice calling him to order.

"Only on the golf course."

"I don't understand."

Never explain a joke. But Philip did cherish the memory of Roger playing wee par golf with great concentration one August evening in Rye. No professional in the final holes of the Masters could have been more focused on what he was doing.

"I wonder if you could come here."

"Here."

Phil was calling from Roger's campus office, which was located in the Brownson Hall whose entrance was flush with the parking lot below Sacred Heart Basilica. The building had served a number of uses in its long career but recently had been converted into offices for lesser faculty and graduate assistants. Father Carmody had resisted Roger's desire to be given an office there.

"You should be with the senior faculty, among the other endowed professors."

Roger gave no indication of any distaste for the professoriate. The mannerisms of the academic acquired over many years struck the outsider as quirky, ranging from what Roger had termed bashful self-assertion to exotic egoism. Of course there were saints as well, but not among the endowed professors. It was not a rank but a status that made the mere full professor somehow less than full. Roger had acquaintances among his fellow endowed professors, even friends, but he felt more affinity with those who, like himself, were relatively new to the academic world, at least to the ranks of the faculty. Convenience apart, and it was a convenience to be able to drop him off almost at the door of his office, the company in Brownson was a stimulant to Roger. Phil explained to Jewel where she would find him and his brother, Roger.

"I thought he was a member of the faculty? He is. I just found him in the phone book."

Was she checking what he said? In principle, Phil approved reasonable caution, but there was an edge to the counselor's voice that suggested disappointment that he was not lying to her.

"One-nineteen Brownson." She was reading from the campus telephone directory.

"That's right."

"You want me to come there?"

"Would you rather have lunch?"

"No, thank you. I never have lunch." A moment ticked by in which her will also ticked. "I will be there."

Phil turned to Roger but his brother had long since lost interest in the phone call. It was Laura's remark that Amanda had visited the counselor in order to lodge a complaint against Pottery that had prompted the invitation to Jewel.

"Phil, Pottery was that ungainly weeping man who showed up that morning at Holy Cross House. He told me all about it. He had hoped to marry the girl."

"Then why would she accuse him of sexual harassment?"

Roger's face puckered in thought. "Philip, I find most males mysterious beyond belief; as for females . . . "

"I want to talk to her."

153

"Do you want me to stay?"

"Roger, this is your office."

The computer that had been provided him here was linked to the network and gave direct access to the main computer, making for far wiser and efficient use than logging on from the apartment via a modem. As a result Roger spent more time on campus than he had planned when they'd remodeled the apartment to accommodate his work and living habits. The thought of writing a book on Maurice Baring was vying with a project involving the American philosopher Charles Sanders Pierce. Roger had invoked him in defense of the oddities of professors, suggesting that weirdness and genius were often near allied, and then having fetched some volumes of Pierce from the library to corroborate his claim become hooked again on the man's writings.

"I haven't read him since graduate school," Roger murmured. "What a mind."

"Can you check out Jewel Fondue, Roger?"

With some reluctance, Roger stored what he was working on and brought up the Notre Dame page. In seconds he had the profile of the counsel or for student complaints on the screen.

"St. Catherine's, B.A., Creighton Law. She has been here five years."

"Single?"

"You'd have to check the campus phone book."

Spouses of faculty and staff were parenthetically listed in the directory. There was no parenthesis behind Jewel Fondue's name.

Having spoken with her on the phone, Phil was prepared for the knuckled announcement of Jewel's arrival.

"Come in," Roger sang out, and the door opened to frame a smallish woman whose hair sprang from her head in groomed disorder. She wore slacks and a fingertip coat and what seemed

154

to be boots, but it was only after she stepped into the room that her disapproving expression was visible.

"Gloria Daley is next door."

"Yes, she is," Roger said, as if delighted by the reminder. "A lovely girl."

Jewel seemed to search the remark for latent condescension. Phil introduced himself and asked her to be seated.

"This office is smaller than mine."

"I have that effect on enclosed spaces," Roger said, but his effort at self-deprecation sailed past her.

"You asked me to come and I have come." The meeting was called to order.

"Laura Flynn mentioned that Amanda Pick had lodged a complaint against Professor Pottery."

"She came to me, yes."

"I am also told that he had proposed marriage."

"The two often go hand in hand."

Roger found that an interesting claim, but Phil headed off a philosophical discussion. Phil had a hunch that the counselor held some form of the view that all sex is rape and that the relation of man to woman is by definition harassing and threatening—the difference between husband and rapist all but erased.

"So you believed her?"

"My first reaction when I heard the dreadful news was to inform the authorities of the danger that Pottery posed to Amanda."

"What authorities?"

"Local. Campus. What is your interest in this?"

"Philip is a detective," Roger said.

"Detective?"

"A private detective," Phil said. "The administration has asked me to conduct a discreet investigation into the unfortunate death of Amanda Pick."

"It could have been prevented. She should have taken action against him."

"Did she refuse to?"

Jewel crossed her hands, uncrossed them, then gripped the arms of the chair she sat in. "She was understandably confused by the situation she was in."

"Do you know Professor Pottery?" Roger asked.

"All too well. He is arrogant. He is pompous. He is fat!" Jewel had crescendoed to this last description, then literally put a hand over her mouth. "Oh, I'm sorry."

"How do you think he feels?" But Roger laughed when he said it. This relaxed the counselor and for the first time she smiled, revealing a pretty and intelligent face.

"Tell us about him," Philip said.

Her profile of the professor was difficult to match with the impressions Phil had gained that morning at Holy Cross House. He remembered the fat man coming clumsily along the lake path, carrying his belly like a burden; he thought of the desolate, self-pitying figure sitting beside Roger on the bench overlooking the lake and later in the refectory of Holy Cross House.

"He was much older than she." The expression of disapproval returned. "More to the point, he was a senior member of the faculty and thick as thieves with members of the tenure committee." She sat back. QED. When there was no immediate response, she sat forward. "You can see the leverage that gave him. There was no need for an explicit threat. The whole situation was threatening. He made his absurd proposal of marriage doubtless counting on being rebuffed, but that would not close the matter. Her fate lay in his hands."

Roger said, "You are giving us reasons why he would *not* have killed her. If he were so determined to make her his wife, he would not have killed her."

"He need not have planned to do it. But it's just because he wanted her so desperately that her refusal would enrage him."

"He seemed a broken man that morning."

"You saw him?"

"Yes."

"At the lake?"

"Yes."

"It's criminal that he should be running around free at the scene of the crime."

"If there was a crime," Roger said.

"If! She is dead, isn't she?"

Roger was stretching a point, at best. Amanda had been asphyxiated and then carried to the lake. If she might conceivably have done the former she could not have done the latter. Throwing a dead body in the lake was in itself a crime even if the one doing so was not responsible for the death; but Roger, knowing as little as he did, could hardly be suggesting that.

The visit from the Counselor for Student Complaints had the negative advantage of making Professor Pottery an unlikely suspect. The thought of the portly professor carrying a dead body down to the lake was as improbable as Roger playing basketball. Nor had he seemed to be a man who shortly before had killed the woman he wanted to marry.

29

HOW CAN A WINTER FUNERAL BE sad? Roger Knight asked himself. The trees were still limned with snow, and the campus streets were shiny black between the heaps of snow that had been cleared from them. The tolling bell of Sacred Heart Basilica, calling such of the faithful as had known her to the final obsequies of Amanda Pick, would in any other season seem lugubrious, but now had a Christmas air. Eternal peace might have been wished upon the departed to the tune of "God Rest You Merry Gentlemen."

"Sad," Philip murmured from the driver's seat. He had found a parking spot on the basketball courts behind the bookstore.

"Yes," Roger said. "But we are not as those who mourn without hope." The scriptural thought seemed to justify his incongruously festive feelings.

They started for the church, Phil's hand under his brother's elbow, lest he hit a slick spot; but if Roger went down, they both went down.

"There's Bridget Quirk," Roger said.

"You're not surprised she's here?"

"Certainly not."

One of the distracting pleasures of the funeral mass was to count the house and take the roll. There was a respectable showing from the Congregation of Holy Cross: the president, his expression a compromise between joy and sorrow; Father Finn bouncing along, thinning hair wild on his narrow head; Father Carmody, of course; and half a dozen elders brought over from Holy Cross House, among them Father Rush. He had the look of a traveler who had missed his flight. The younger priests were assistant deans or hall rectors, and, of course, there was Bishop Jenky, member of the Congregation of Holy Cross, auxiliary to the bishop of Fort Wayne–South Bend. His beaming countenance cast a bearded benediction from left to right in synchrony with his triply blessing hand. The lay faculty were already scattered in the pews, cheek by jowl with graduate students and even some lesser entities. In the east transept was a representation of *emeriti,* including Gleason and O'Connell, there if for no other reason than a dress rehearsal. Is this how it would be when they too shuffled off this mortal coil?

"Dying during midsemester break or a vacation is inadvisable," Father Carmody had informed Roger. "And summer? Disaster. A graveside ceremony would suffice."

"You mean student attendance is down?"

"Oh no, no. Students almost never come to funerals. But when the faculty is all here and on campus, many are bound to show up."

"Ah."

"Weather can be a factor, too."

"Surely this snow won't affect the funeral."

"Not even the grave digging. But I remember George Shuster."

George Shuster, a Domer who had taught a few years at Notre Dame after graduation before going on to great success in the wider world, including the presidency of Hunter College, had returned to Notre Dame in his golden years as a special assistant to Father Hesburgh.

"An honorary post?"

"Not at all. He had his finger in many pies. His office was on the eleventh floor of the library, and he was in it nearly every day."

"He died in winter?"

"In the middle of a week-long blizzard. The campus roads

were like tunnels between the piled-up snow. A stiff wind brought down branches on which ice had formed. It gave new meaning to deciduous. The temperature was ten below. What would have been one of the great funerals passed like a well-kept secret."

"I suppose he would have been willing to wait until spring."

"He should have," Father Carmody said, detecting no irony in the observation.

It was a pleasant thought that the size of attendance at one's funeral depended on so many irrelevancies. Certainly Amanda was sent on her way in more than respectable fashion. But she was to be buried in California, so things came to a halt on the road outside the main entrance of the basilica where the coffin was slid into a hearse and the door closed on it.

Father Finn came up to Roger. "Would you and your brother care for lunch?"

"Absolutely."

"I've made a reservation at the Morris Inn."

"There will be others?"

"Professor Pottery."

"I warn you, I'm starved," Roger said. "Funerals make me ravenous."

Father Finn did not take this amiss, welcoming what in the circumstances might have seemed unwonted levity. But they hung about for some minutes, looking and being looked at. An abject Pottery stood with his overcoat unbuttoned and his stomach on display, weeping openly, but attracting no attention. Roger noticed the familiar faces of policemen. Father Rush wandered away from his group, a scarf dangling from his neck like a wooly stole. He stared at Roger, then came toward him, moving on a bias.

"I am Father Rush," he announced.

"I remember you."

"Where did we meet?"

"Outside Holy Cross House, the morning they found the body."

"It's a good morning when there's no body."

"I meant the lady in the lake."

Father Rush thought about it.

"I meant the lady for whom the funeral mass was just said."

Father Rush stepped back and looked at Roger with sudden recollection in his watery eyes. "We sat on the bench."

"You talked of the missions."

"Someone kept interrupting."

He was delighted with his ability to recall the occasion and looked around as if for applause.

"Come to lunch," Father Rush said, not seeming to include his confrere, Father Finn, in the invitation.

"I would love to, but I can't today."

"Come any day."

"Thank you, Father. I will."

"We like guests."

"Who doesn't?"

"I didn't know the deceased."

"She was a junior faculty member."

"Imagine, throwing her in the lake like that. And they say the pagans have no respect for life. I was in the missions."

"Bangladesh?"

"How did you know."

But he was taken away then by a nurse who insisted on apologizing for Father Rush.

"We're good friends," Roger assured her.

"He's coming to lunch," Father Rush said.

She brightened. "Today?"

"Soon."

Her expression suggested that she thought this was the usual put-off of the elderly and Roger wanted to insist that he meant it, that he would be coming to Holy Cross House for lunch as soon as he could. But it was too late; Father Rush was being shuffled back to the contingent from the retirement home to be bussed back into oblivion.

The Morris Inn had a valedictory air. The campus hotel was to be replaced by a more ample structure and would be remodeled for some other use. Since coming here, the Knight brothers had come to like the dining room of the inn, almost preferring it to the University Club in the evenings. Despite the fine cuisine and pleasant surroundings, the restaurant was seldom crowded and it was possible to prolong one's meal for hours. The staff seemed delighted rather than annoyed by this, perhaps dreading finding themselves alone. However attractive its proposed successor, nothing could possibly replace the Morris Inn in the affection of generations of students and faculty and alumni. Now at noon there was a crowd, and it was well that Father Finn had taken the precaution of making a reservation.

As they were being shown to a table by the window, they passed Wendy Schlereth, the head archivist, seated with a young man. Her brows lifted in greeting but she did not speak lest she interrupt what the young man was saying to her. It was only when he had passed the table that Roger saw it was Noah. Were they discussing the Henry Horan papers?

"I'm glad she isn't being buried here," Phil said. "It makes it seem less definitive."

"I thought it was a splendid ceremony," Roger said.

"I didn't know you ranked funerals."

"I appreciate a well-done liturgy," Father Carmody said.

"Still, it's so sad. I keep thinking of the work she was doing that was not yet done, that now will never be done."

"The same might have been true if she'd died fifty years from now."

"Died. I noticed that no one drew attention to how she had died."

Roger began to ruminate on a possible liturgy for victims of

163

murder, on an analogy with the feasts of martyrs, a whole array of options to cover the different ways in which people met their deaths. Mass for a homicide. Perhaps another for a heterocide.

"There'll be one for a pesticide if you don't cut it out," Phil said. And then Professor Pottery joined them.

He had given up his overcoat but not his stricken countenance. He moved through the tables like a steel ball maneuvering through a pinball machine, his head thrown back so that he could avail himself of the glasses that had slipped, as usual, to the end of his nose. The smell of strong drink preceded him. Obviously he had stopped in the bar across from the restaurant.

"I should fly to California with the body," he said, taking a chair.

"Your own?" Roger asked.

"Nonsense," said Father Carmody.

Pottery looked at Roger wildly. "You don't know what it's like."

Flying to California? Roger let it go. How long would this valedictory mood persist? Sean had loved Amanda but she had not loved him in turn; and this meant, if Plato is right in the *Lysis,* that they were not even friends let alone affianced. It did not seem right to mourn an unrealized possibility with the thoroughness that Pottery was doing.

"She would have wanted you to be strong," Roger lied.

"I may ask for early retirement."

"That would be very unwise. What would you do all day?"

"I ask myself the same question. The empty days stretch before me . . . "

He emitted a prolonged and alcohol-scented sigh. "Let's have a drink."

Phil approved of this as did Father Finn and soon they had ordered. Roger would have coffee.

30

Father Carmody offered to take Roger to his office. Roger
looked ruefully at the diminutive car to which Father Carmody
led him. "I don't think I'll fit."

"It's a lot bigger than it looks."

"So am I."

The front passenger seat was pushed as close to the wind-
shield as it would go, thus enlarging the backseat area. The
door, of course, remained the same width, and it was only with
great effort and a rather insistent push by Father Carmody that
Roger eventually found himself wedged in the back seat. His
head was bent forward, and he could feel the curve of the roof
against the back of his head. His arms hung between his legs so
as to lessen his width.

"Okay?" Father Carmody asked.

"Never better," Roger said. His voice seemed squeezed
from his contracted body.

Father Carmody drove as one who has here no lasting city,
seeming to delight when the car went into a skid so that he could
display his winter driving skills to the maximum. The knack
was to turn into the skid, not away from it. Roger doubted that
he would ever have a use for this lore. When Father Carmody
spun into the parking lot below Sacred Heart Basilica that
abutted Brownson Hall where Roger's office was, it was hard not
to emit a cheer of relief.

"Come in," Roger said, when he had been pried and pulled

from the backseat and stood in the snowy parking lot, arms akimbo, stamping his feet.

"I will. There is a favor I must ask you."

"I am at your command."

This risky acquiescence was justified by the sequel. Father Carmody wanted Roger to have a talk with Noah, and he proposed that the three of them have lunch together.

"I know Noah."

"I'm aware of that. That's why I think you can be of help to us on this."

"What exactly is *this?*"

"Why don't we save all that for lunch."

"Where will it be?"

"The Morris Inn. I'll come for you." Noting Roger's look of dismay, he added, "In one of the university's limousines."

They parted at the door of Roger's office. With the door closed, his computer on, and settled in a chair for which his bulk was not an uneven challenge, he emitted a sigh. His normal reaction when settling into his office for the day was to breathe a prayer of thanksgiving to the providence that had brought him to Notre Dame. Here he was able to pursue such pursuits as he wished and to offer a course each semester that fell under the rather commodious title of his endowed chair, Catholic Studies. Roger had the convert's confidence that everything was related to Catholicism in one way or the other. But this semester he was discussing the works of James Huneker, the man for whom his chair was named.

But how on this morning could he get his mind off the fact that Amanda Pick was dead, the victim of foul play, just as the time for a decision on her tenure approached? The thought had crossed his mind, before he knew the particulars of her death, that Amanda had learned what the committee's vote would be and, despondent, had headed for the lake and oblivion.

31

with Fathers Finn and Carmody and Noah Beispiel, the Saint Louis bookdealer Roger had met in the archives, was a complete change of pace from the somber events of the past days. These sad matters were not quite irrelevant to the point of the luncheon, however. Nor did Father Finn postpone business until they had eaten. As soon as they had given the waitress their orders, the associate provost said to Noah, "Why don't you bring the others up to speed on your proposal."

"I made this proposal before the unfortunate death of the woman who discovered the manuscript."

"But you haven't withdrawn it."

Noah winced. "No. No, I haven't. The offer still stands."

Noah professed to have been as surprised as anyone when the unpublished Father Brown story was found. It was his contention that the story had been among the few manuscripts that Henry Horan had bequeathed to his alma mater. "It was included among them by mistake."

"But it was not found in the cartons containing the Ryan papers."

"It would be more correct to say that it was not put in storage with the rest of the donation."

"Is that conjecture?"

"Not anymore. Greg Whelan told me that he deliberately put it among the papers that record the history of *Scholastic Magazine*. He connected it with a contest that had been sponsored to see what student could best mimic the style of Chesterton."

Father Finn said, "You mean that Whelan thought it was a student production?"

"Perhaps," Noah said, and then let a little silence grow before speaking again. "In any case, that is why Amanda Pick discovered the story. She rightly saw that it was an original. I think you verified that for her, Roger."

"It would have been obvious to anyone who had seen samples of Chesterton's handwriting."

"Even to Whelan?" Father Carmody asked.

Roger intervened. "So it is your contention that the story was not meant to be included in the gift of Horan papers."

"I am certain it was not."

"How?"

Their food arrived then, but the conversation went on over the arm of the waitress, around her, and continued as they ate. Noah might have welcomed the semiinterruption.

"I bought Henry Horan's papers at auction. The lot was described as containing all his papers."

"Except those he donated to the university?"

"*All* his papers."

"So you are representing yourself and not the Horan estate."

"As far as his papers go, I *am* the Horan estate."

"And you wish to make a claim on the manuscript?"

Father Finn shook his head vigorously. "It's not that simple."

"When I came here, it was with the idea of making a gift to the university of all of Henry Horan's papers. His devotion to, almost obsession with Notre Dame, seemed to dictate that."

"Obsession?" Father Carmody repeated. "He all but ignored the place throughout his lifetime."

"It was never out of his thoughts. I have his diary."

"Is that among the things you intended to give to the archives?"

"Intend to give. But in the light of recent developments, there is a condition. When I sent off the Horan papers that are now in possession of the university, it was with the express description that these were papers of Henry Horan."

"How did he come into possession of the Chesterton story?" Roger asked.

Noah had done little more than pick at his food, but he had drunk three glasses of water since they sat down at the table. "That is an interesting story."

As Noah told it, Henry Horan had asked the famous author if he could have some memento of his stay at Notre Dame. Chesterton, aware of the imitation Chesterton contest that Henry had induced the *Scholastic* to run, offered to give his young fan the manuscript of a Father Brown story he had actually written at Notre Dame.

"And never published?"

"Apparently not. But it was a gift to Henry Horan. He did not give the boy publication rights to the story."

What Noah proposed seemed very generous. He wanted to reclaim the Chesterton story, but he would pay a sum of money for it. Besides, he would make the donation of the remaining Henry Horan papers that he had already all but promised. Father Finn expressed his sense that this was a very reasonable proposal.

"With one exception. I don't think we should ask Noah to pay in order to get back something that, according to his argument, was never meant to be given in the first place."

Father Carmody nodded his agreement.

"Roger," Father Finn said, "what do you think the reaction in the archives would be?"

"About waiving payment? I doubt they would have an opinion on that." Roger looked at Noah. "Henry Horan's diaries would be included in your gift?"

Noah hesitated. "Of course." He moved a spoon about on the tablecloth. "But out of deference to those still living whom he writes about, I think they should be embargoed for, say, twenty-five years."

Roger emitted a theatrical groan. "I don't think I can wait twenty-five years to read them."

"Henry Horan was an interesting fellow," Carmody agreed. "I would like to learn what estranged him from Notre Dame, but I don't have another twenty-five years so I suppose I'll have to ask him in person."

"Don't overestimate the interest of the diaries," Noah said. "Eighty percent of the entries date from his time as a student."

"That is exactly what interests me," Roger said.

"How so?"

"He ran the Chesterton imitation contest."

"The thing was his idea."

"I wonder if he recorded his conversations with Chesterton about it. Wasn't Chesterton going to be one of the judges?"

"I don't remember much on that," Noah said.

"You've read the diaries?" Father Finn asked. He had the expression of a man who thought a conversation had disappeared up a tangent and might never return.

"More or less."

They adjourned on a note of agreement, and later in the archives, when Roger passed on the results of the meeting—the question about the reaction in the archives seemed to justify this—Whelan was struck dumb in his eagerness to say something. Wendy sipped her coffee and Roger looked away, and then the words came.

"That's a damned lie. The story was included in the papers Henry Horan gave."

"But did he know he gave it?"

"It was the one thing he mentioned specifically in his covering letter."

"Where is that?"

It was in the first archival box still in storage in the basement of Holy Cross House. Roger and Whelan went immediately to get it.

"That would change the agreement we made at lunch," Roger said.

The cover letter from Henry Horan was not in any of the three boxes in storage at Holy Cross House.

32

HARVEY MICHAELS WAS A BEARDED
public relations man, whose loyalty to the university was unrivaled. Harvey had hitched his star to Notre Dame, returning to work for the university after a stint in the outside world, and now he had been too long in the comparatively still waters of academe to contemplate reentry into the swift and competitive currents of off-campus life. That is how he still mentally divided reality—campus and off-campus. His life was entirely on: He had a room on the second floor of the firehouse, he ate in the campus dining halls, he drank in the Morris Inn or the University Club, he attended daily mass at 11:30 in Sacred Heart Basilica. Kneeling there among a smattering of students, he could close his eyes and believe that nothing had changed since he was eighteen years old.

But of course the university had changed immeasurably since he had been a student. Sacred Heart might look pretty much as it had then—although Bishop Jenky had brought it back to its nineteenth-century splendor when he was rector of the basilica—and a dozen other buildings seemed unchanged. But even in permanence there was change, if only the changes required to make it appear that no change had occurred. What building had not been remodeled at least once since his student days? The Main Building had received a thorough overhaul. It looked the same outside, it was familiar enough within, but Harvey had the sense he'd had in Disney World. Then he had been almost surprised to look up and see that the sky was real. But even if the core of the traditional campus had been left untouched, it now existed in a setting of new buildings that made it seem another place.

Harvey had explained all this to Phil, and Phil had passed it on to Roger. "He is a congenial character," Roger had said.

He was also convivial, at least late in the day when he was at his table in the bar of the Morris Inn or riding a stool in the back bar at the University Club. In the former place, Harvey paid due deference to the well-ensconced Professor Pottery and thus elicited from the sage memorable remarks, nostalgic souvenirs, and a veritable narrative flow in which the past had the benefit of Pottery's shaping imagination. In the club bar the conversation turned on sports, but Harvey was a Renaissance man whose antennae could vibrate to the literary or to the athletic with equal ease. Father Finn was right to think that any bad news about Notre Dame would be in good hands with Harvey Michaels.

"It is difficult to tell whether the news is good or bad, Roger."

"Phil, a murder on the campus is already bad news. Not that it has never happened before. A little lady named Dorry, who frequents the archives, has gathered a remarkable sheaf of material on strange campus deaths over the past century and a half."

"Roy Gross has talked to Pottery, but now he is pretty well determined to pursue that vigorously."

"What do you think of that?"

"It is difficult imagining Pottery doing anything strenuous."

The conversation between Harvey and Roger culminated in an effort to summarize what had happened and what was known over the past two days.

- On Tuesday morning, at about 7:00 A.M., Blanche Crowley discovered the dead body of Amanda Pick, half submerged in Saint Joseph's Lake.

174

- Perhaps an hour prior to that, Fr. Matthew Rush, from his bench on the front lawn of Holy Cross House, which gave him an excellent view of the golden dome and the spire of Sacred Heart as well as of the lake and the path that ran below the house, watched someone carry a burden down to the lake. That person returned unburdened.

- The time of death had been set at perhaps two hours before discovery, which would mean an hour before the body was deposited in the lake.

- Whoever brought the body could have parked a vehicle in the parking lot of Holy Cross House and then carried it down to the lake.

"Was it a man or woman, Father?"

"Wasn't she a teacher in the philosophy department?"

"I mean the one who carried the body."

"Who knows the way people dress anymore. Whoever it was had a woolen hat pulled down tight."

"Heavy or light? And I don't mean the hat," Phil added.

Father Rush smiled. "Everyone looks overweight to me since my years in Bangladesh."

"But the person was overweight?"

"For a Bangladeshi."

"Was it a Bangladeshi?"

"I am making a comparison. I can't imagine any of the people in my mission doing a thing like this."

- Amanda Pick had been wearing a hooded jacket that belonged to Laura Flynn. This startling fact had a flood of implications and related comments.

- Amanda had never before jogged, so far as Laura knew.

- Despite this, the two women borrowed one another's clothes frequently; and if Amanda had impulsively

175

decided to go jogging, it would not be surprising that she had put on Laura's jacket.

- One consequence of this fact was the possibility that Amanda had been mistaken for Laura, and Laura was the intended victim.

- Militating against that possibility was the fact that the murder had not been committed on the lake path but elsewhere, with the body being brought to the lake about an hour after the crime was committed. That put the time of death at five o'clock.

"Wasn't that early for her to be up and around?"

"Normally, yes. But she was so keyed up over the coming tenure decision that she had not been sleeping well."

"But you didn't hear her go out?"

"When I heard the news that something had happened to Amanda, my first thought was to dismiss it. I just assumed she was still in her room."

"Who usually got up first in the morning, you or Amanda?"

"That depended on the day. If I had an early class, I got going before seven."

"How about Tuesday?"

"I have a Tuesday morning class."

"Did you yourself jog on Tuesdays?"

"When I have a morning class, I substitute the NordicTrack for running."

"The NordicTrack?"

"It's an exercise machine that simulates cross-country skiing. I'm from Minnesota."

"Did you jog on Monday?"

"This semester I run every day but Tuesday and Thursday."

"Did you have exercise Tuesday morning?"

"I never miss."

"Could someone enter the house when you're exercising?"

"And me not hear? The machine makes noise and I watch television."

"So someone could have entered the house?"

"Someone did."

"Someone?"

"Professor Pottery."

"But how would he get into the house?"

"When he is drunk, he is capable of anything."

- At first Raoul had told the police that Professor Pottery had left the Morris Inn in his usual advanced condition of drunkenness at the usual time, that is, one-thirty in the morning. He later changed half of that. He had left drunk but before midnight.

- Gross had learned of the 7-Eleven where Pottery often stopped on his way home, his usual need a six-pack of beer. Neither of the two people who had been on duty remembered what Pottery had bought. When they said beer, they were answering from past performance.

- There was at least the logical possibility that Laura had killed her housemate.

"I mean her statement does not contradict the possibility that she did it" Roger explained.

"What's her motive?"

"Phil, I don't mean that it is likely, plausible, or probable, only that it is logically possible."

"Is that supposed to make sense?"

"Trust me."

"I'd have to."

"Go back to your summary."

"What time did you get up on Tuesday morning, Professor Pottery?"

"I didn't. It was afternoon before I got out of bed."

"Did you ask him when he went to bed, Phil?"

"I wish you'd been there, Roger. I find it hard to get a straight answer out of the guy."

- Pottery's unusually late arising on Tuesday could be explained by his having been up until dawn.

"Killing girls and carrying their bodies to the lake."

"Only one."

"Do you believe he did that?"

"It's logically possible."

"Meaning it's illogical to think so."

"Not quite."

"How about Fred Cossette?"

"Fred Cossette?"

"He dates Laura."

"I know who he is, Roger."

- Fred Cossette had been in Chicago for the weekend and had not returned until late Monday, when he went to bed early. He had not been up and about on Tuesday until after he heard the news of Amanda's death on the radio.

- Hans Wiener had his hands full with his young family. He dressed the twins and fed them their breakfast so that his wife, Teresa, could enjoy an extra hour after nursing the baby.

"And so, Roger," Phil concluded, "the police have decided to go with Sean Pottery."

"I suppose they can hardly be blamed."

"So what do you think?"

"I think it is absurd to suspect Pottery of this. Not because he might not have motivation or reason or unreason enough to do it, but because he is physically incapable of it. Still, lying to the police was dumb."

"Lying?"

"About when he got up on Tuesday morning. He was at the scene of the crime before nine."

Phil thought about that. "Maybe he hadn't been to bed yet."

33

engaged to be married, the date for the wedding all set, and he
and his fiancée embarked on a marriage preparation course.
And then she had left town to visit her aunt. That is why the letter came from Cincinnati. She had decided that she didn't want
to get married. She had tried several times to tell him this face
to face, but her nerve always failed her and that is why she was
resorting to this letter. It went on and on, pages in which she
told him how hard it was for her to tell him this. Had he ever
finished reading that interminably self-pitying letter? He was
shattered. The task of explaining that there would be no wedding was left to Fred. He left town himself, heading north to
South Bend.

That broken engagement and aborted wedding had left a
permanent scar. For a long time, Fred privately observed the
anniversary of the marriage that had not been. He floundered.
If the marriage had taken place as planned, he would have gone
on working in the printing room of the Nashville paper. He
remembered how he had calculated his slow rise through the
ranks and imagined himself one day the senior man on his
shift. A whole imagined life that had never been.

A printer can find work anywhere, and Fred found work in
South Bend. But it was lonely. He began to read a lot. He had
always enjoyed reading, but there had been no plan or method
in it. Now he was working his way through the one hundred
Great Books, and reading books about them by Mortimer Adler.
He found himself craving to know the meaning of life. What

had happened to him lent urgency to the question. He signed up for courses at Indiana University South Bend and got hooked. He switched to the graveyard shift and enrolled full time and got his B.A. in three years. He wanted to go on and do graduate work, but whenever he brought it up, his age became a topic with the professor. Fred began to see that professors did not like their occupation being treated as a second career. He applied for admission to the graduate school at Notre Dame with the same attitude that he bought tickets to the lottery. He had never won the lottery, but his application was successful.

Pride gave way to the realization that his grasp was not quite as extensive as his reach. The classes were far more demanding than anything he had taken hitherto. There were days when the only sensible thing seemed to be to admit defeat and go back to the printing trade. He had the impression that other students were not experiencing his difficulties, which seemed another reason to call it quits. And then one day he ran into Professor Flynn in the Huddle, and she asked him to have coffee with her. When she asked him how things were going, he blurted out all his doubts.

"Fred, you wouldn't have been admitted if you weren't capable of the work."

She seemed genuinely concerned to allay his doubts, and over two cups of coffee she sought to encourage him by telling him how difficult she herself had found graduate work. "For extrinsic reasons, in large part. But not entirely. Like you, I was a little older than the other students."

That chat was the first of many. Laura—he didn't call her that for some months—made him a special project and wanted regular progress reports. He became a regular at her office, and often they had lunch in the Decio sandwich bar.

"Are students allowed in here?"

"As guests. No one would think you're a student anyway."

"Sometimes I feel the same way."

Her laughter did not come easily, but when she did laugh

it transformed her. When she talked about her involvement in women's affairs, her face seemed thin and cheerless. Eventually she told him of her marriage, of her husband's opposition to her studies, of his doing everything to oppose and discourage it, of the annulment. As quid pro quo, he told her of the wedding that never was.

"She just called it off?"

"In a letter."

"No."

It was the first time he was willing to receive sympathy for his plight. It was what friends and relatives would have said by way of consolation that had made him decide to leave Nashville. With Laura it was different. Her own experience gave her the right to say what she did. She even smiled when he told her he had as much against women as she did against men.

"But it's not really the same," she said.

"I suppose not."

They had dinner a few times, went to movies in the auditorium of the museum. One night she did not immediately open the door when he pulled up in front of her place. They talked a bit. Silence fell. He wasn't sure what her reaction would be when he put his hand on hers. She turned toward him immediately, and then his lips were crushing hers.

But after mere moments, she pushed him away and turned from him and began to cry. When he put a hand on her shoulder, she shrugged it away. "Laura, I'm sorry. You mustn't think that . . ."

"Mustn't think what?"

But he no longer knew what he had meant to say, if he ever had.

"I don't hate men, Fred. I don't. It's just that . . . "

"Just what?"

"Now I'm doing it." Her eyes glistened with tears as she smiled at him. "It's just that I still feel married."

She ran through her sad story again, bitterness coming and

going, but her bafflement and anger at what had happened to her was an aphrodisiac and soon her lips were pressed to his again. When she broke free this time, it was clearly out of fear that they would go too far. He took her to the door, where they stood facing one another, very close. She leaned her forehead against his chin, and the closeness and silence seemed all they wanted.

"Thank you, Fred."

"Thank you."

When he got behind the wheel of his car, he noticed that there was someone sitting in the parked car across the street and facing the opposite way. It was a man and he was looking at Fred. Some lonely guy who had witnessed the tender good-bye? Fred felt sorry for him. He waved.

The car's window rolled down and for a moment Fred had an impression of the man in the driver street. And then he noticed the gun. Or did he hear it go off before he noticed it? The glass of the back windows of his car shattered, and shards of it went spinning about. Fred was grazed by pieces of it; a sliver stuck in the back of his neck. Meanwhile, the other car left in a roar, and Fred sat there in the once more silent street, feeling blood trickling down the back of his neck.

There was a flood of light as Laura's door opened. She was silhouetted against the lighted hallway and then began to move tentatively toward him. Fred scrambled out of his car and ran toward her. "Go inside. He might come back!"

"What happened? Oh, my God, you're bleeding."

She led him into the house and into the kitchen, placing him in a chair with his back to the sink and tended to his dozen wounds.

"This may hurt," she said, before removing a sliver of glass, but he was numb. All he could think of was that a man had pointed a gun at him and fired. Laura asked him what had happened, and he gave her an account that seemed wholly inadequate to the incredible fact that someone had just apparently tried to kill him.

"Did you see who it was?"

"It was nobody I know."

"What did he look like?"

It should have been easy to describe the man, the image of him was still so vivid in Fred's mind, but he found himself incapable even of beginning. Why would anyone want to kill him? Laura let it go and worked in silence, dabbing an astringent on the smaller wounds with wads of cotton, putting Band-Aids over larger wounds. Once she leaned over and rested her cheek on the top of his head. Fred felt a wave of tenderness go through him. When she was done, Laura left the kitchen and when she came back she was carrying an album. She plucked it down on the kitchen table and opened it.

"Was this the man who shot at you?"

He got up and looked down at the page of snapshots. Laura was in some of them and a man. Fred leaned down to look more closely. He stood up.

"Who is he?"

"My husband. Was he the man?"

"Yes."

34

ONE OF THE REASONS THAT PRO-
fessor Pottery loved Chesterton was that Chesterton loved Dickens. *Bleak House* was Pottery's favorite. It had everything—a
beautifully complicated plot, sentimentality, grotesques, comic
characters, unforgettable scenes, and running through it all the
endless case of *Jarndyce versus Jarndyce,* rendering futile the
efforts of the majority of the characters. Pottery had come to see
that the endless and insoluble lawsuit was a symbol of life.
Novels have plots, beginnings, middles, and ends; but a human
life is a sequence of actions whose real meaning is not what
they aim at but what they are. It is a difficult thing for one
whose passion is literature to realize that a story inevitably dis-
torts life by giving it an intelligible completeness.

"I am not a novel," Pottery would inform himself in his
waking mirror. And at night, he would drunkenly proclaim, "It
is you who have thickened, not the plot."

The criteria of real acts is their moral quality. Sean Pottery
had come to realize this obvious truth by a very circuitous
route. But now that he knew it, it was a judgment on him rather
than a consolation. The façade he had developed for the world
made him a kind of model of deportment, like Dickens's Mr.
Turveydrop. His outer had nothing to do with his inner. Within,
he knew with bitter certainty that he was a fraud and a joke.
His professorial persona was an escape, a pose, an imposture.
The Chesterton he loved was a judgment on him. Everything he
loved was a judgment on him. He fell short of every ideal he
espoused.

He had cast himself in the role of the Notre Dame don, one of that long and noble tradition of dedicated teachers who had eschewed marriage and lived a lay but almost clerical life, always at the disposal of their students. On days when his self-disgust was less acute, he might allow that to some degree he had achieved this ideal. But he had done so by turning himself into a curmudgeon, a tyrant, a martinet. The students who were impressed, those who when they had graduated kept the newsletter going, were not the best students. The truly good students eluded him. Those who professed to admire him had little grasp of Chesterton or anyone else. He was good theater and they admired him, far more as the distance between themselves and the campus increased than when they were actual spectators. Sean Pottery regarded his very popularity as a teacher as fraudulent.

When Amanda had first come to him, he had reacted in character and for a time she had been amused and attracted by this persona that was not, he was certain, himself. He saw in her fresh and intelligent youth the path he had not taken and which suddenly seemed irresistibly attractive. Why had he not married and had a family and lived a life that was more than his professorial career? As he was, there was nothing of him beyond the campus. He was a nonperson everywhere but in the familiar setting that had contained him for a quarter of a century. Amanda reminded him that there might have been more.

Was it too late? He tried to drop his mannerisms and speak to her from the heart, but he could not do it. Only when she sat with him at his table in the Morris Inn and the drinks kept coming could he begin to imitate his real self. But she had tired of those hours spent in a bar. He knew it was a stupid practice, but it was what he had become. A semester ended and she had ceased to be his drinking companion. She was even more powerfully present to him in her absence. Amanda became his obsession.

Finally, with the Dutch courage of alcohol, he called at her door late, drunk, amorous, certain that now he could speak to her as he wanted to. He had made a dreadful ass of himself. His cheeks burned with shame when in the sober daylight he recalled what he had done. What hurt most was the thought that she had misunderstood his intentions. His must have seemed a mere animal passion to her when the truth was that for the first time in his life he was feeling the power of selfless love. Like a young man, he wanted to do dangerous and brave things for her; he wanted to be her hero. And all he was was a drunken senior colleague showing up at all hours and making a fool of himself.

He had been educated by Benedictines. Occasionally, he went off to Saint Anselm's in Manchester, New Hampshire, and made a retreat. He had put himself under the spiritual direction of Father John. In the manner of fitful penitents, he'd felt the tug of the religious life and felt a fugitive desire to stay permanently with the monks, become a monk himself. What else was he, anyway? Sitting in the choir while the community chanted the office, the chaste neums establishing themselves one after another in the incensed air, rising and falling on a diminishing scale, the absurdity of his life seemed manifest. To recall in those surroundings his drunken visit to Amanda's door in the middle of the night was particularly penitential.

He returned to Notre Dame with his spiritual batteries charged. It was doubtless impossible at this stage of his career to abandon the personage he had become, but as between himself and God it was understood that this was but a semblance, a shell, a patina, beneath which the real and never-to-be-observed Sean Pottery dwelt, a simple man, straightforward, of few words. And so he carried on for a time, like a drunk between toots, but eventually he fell and presented himself again in an advanced intoxicated state at Amanda Pick's door. She was not at home, but he was ushered in by her housemate. In the blurred memories he carried away of what then transpired, it seemed to Pottery that this woman, Laura Flynn, had accosted him on the couch and reacted to him as he had

189

dreamed of the divine Amanda reacting. He had fled in terror from the Jezebel.

It was on a subsequent bibulous evening that he had decided that there was but one honorable course of action. He must propose marriage to Amanda. This would sweep away any equivocation that might have attended his earlier clumsy advances. She would understand the seriousness of his intentions. And her housemate, who apparently thought he was a rampant animal for whom any female of the species was as good as another, would also grasp the lay of the land. He composed a letter. He destroyed it. He labored over another. That too ended up a rejected wad in his fireplace. What was wanted was nature, not art. He must speak from the heart. He put aside his jumbo fountain pen, an instrument he had flourished so often it had become a sort of symbol of him, picked up a ballpoint, and dashed off a note to Amanda, asking that she marry him lest he go mad. He struck the addendum but did not rewrite the note. Off it went, the die was cast, his fate was in her hands.

Some time later, before he had received a reply, a woman he did not know and of whose function in the university he had been unaware, came to him, sitting herself at his table in the Morris Inn bar where he was seeking in the grape some diversion from his mental agony. He listened to her in disbelief and treated her as she deserved. He dashed his drink in her face and had Raoul remove her from the premises.

"Sexual harassment." The very phrase had an ideological ring that revealed itself to be one of the inventions of recent times as a substitute for the morality that had been tossed aside. Females wished to labor cheek by jowl with males; they aspired to the alleged sexual irresponsibility of the male, aided in this by chemicals that doubtless distorted their psyches as well as their bodies; they flaunted their charms and then expressed surprise if the signals they sent were received and responded to. The watchword was "consent." Nothing of itself was good or bad but the consent that made it so. Pottery's only regret was that the woman had chosen to harass him when he had already finished half his drink and thus could douse her only with what remained.

It was the ultimate insult to speak of his elevated and sublime feelings for Amanda in feminist jargon. While he awaited her reply to his letter, he was conscious of how the tenure decision weighed on her mind. How he longed to tell her that she need not fret about the outcome of that benighted committee's considerations. As the wife of Prof. Sean Pottery she could retire from the classroom to the cultivated leisure she deserved. He wanted to provide her with comfort and security. He wished to become her slave.

And then, after her cruel death, the awful accusations once more came, but this time publicly. He had no doubt who the source of such slander was. He could still see her wide, flat face running with his drink. He would deal with her again. What was her name? Opal? Gemma? Sapphire? Jewel? That was it, Jewel Fondue. Pottery called for the Notre Dame directory in order to locate this female who had the effrontery to libel him to the world.

mind to creative heights as he wrote the announcement of the
generous donation of Noah Beispiel, a cache of papers amassed
over the years by a son of Notre Dame, who throughout a long
life never lost the boyish ardor instilled in him as an athlete
and a scholar on campus.

Harvey paused. *Oh, for a muse of fire.* Oh, for a match was
more like it. He highlighted what he had written and pressed
Del. Just like that the screen of his monitor was blank. Harvey
missed the satisfaction of tearing a sheet of paper from the
typewriter, crushing it into a ball, and sailing it in the general
direction of a wastebasket. The computer eliminated almost all
of the irksome, habit-forming, somehow lovable burden of writing. Mechanical typewriters had called for actual physical
effort. The keys had to be struck forcibly, driving them down in
order to make the steel letters bang against the inky ribbon and
impress itself on the paper rolled round the patten of the
machine. The writer turned finally away from his Underwood or
Royal or Smith Corona with stiff fingers and aching neck, a
day's work done. The electric typewriter had eliminated the
need to return the carriage manually at the end of a line. Harvey thought of it as analogous to the transition from the stick
shift to automatic transmission. A limping analogy. Easier it
might be, but it was still driving a car. The computer was an
entirely different mode of transportation. No paper. Constant
rewriting. The ability to shift paragraphs around. Spell checking. How could you work up a sweat with such a method?

Finally, one punched another key and the whole text emerged from the printer, uniformly printed, no darker or lighter letters.

When Harvey's mind wandered to the medium, he knew something was wrong with the message. Why had Father Finn insisted on a particularly fulsome acknowledgment of the Noah Beispiel bequest?

"Pull out all the stops," Finn had urged Harvey, then looked puzzled. "What does that mean, anyway?"

"Pulling out all the stops?"

"Yes."

"I'll look it up."

It seemed to have something to do with the pipe organ, but the explanation Harvey had found presupposed a good deal of knowledge of the instrument. If he had that, he would not have had to look up "stops" in the dictionary and then go on to the encyclopedia. He had decided not to call Father Finn about it. Chances were the associate provost's wonderment had been a passing thing.

The Beispiel Bequest was already a misnomer. The papers involved were those of Henry Horan, a bona fide alumnus. More important still, most of the stuff donated concerned Chesterton. What more obvious than that he should consult Pottery, one of the few professors Harvey was sure he would have remembered if he had continued his career in the outer world. Pottery was fun drunk or sober and there were times of the day when it was impossible to know which he was.

Harvey expected to find Pottery at his usual table in the bar of the Morris Inn, but he was not there, and Raoul the bartender only shrugged and looked forlorn when Harvey asked him where Pottery was. It turned out that he was at home. The man who came to the door was one who had been altered by recent events. Pottery had actually shown up at the lakeside before Amanda's body was taken away. He had figured in the newspaper coverage of that startling death, portrayed as a tragi-comic figure, an old man with a hopeless crush on a much younger woman.

"Have all the laws of libel become obsolete?" Pottery demanded of Harvey.

"I'm not a lawyer."

"Who said that the female franchise, plus instantaneous electronic communication, would spell the end of the country the Founders had in mind?"

"I don't know."

"I did!"

This bravura pronouncement would once have been adequately prepared for, a fanfare introducing it. "Males of the species are in the main mad, but females are hysterical. It is one thing for that wench to accuse me unjustly to my face; it is quite another when she takes her lies to the media."

"We are speaking of Jewel Fondue?"

"Unfortunately. But necessarily."

"Apparently Amanda Pick filed a complaint against you at her office."

"I don't believe that for a minute."

"I have seen it."

Pottery did not lose a beat. "Doubtless a fabrication by that mad woman. She is, in Aristotle's phrase, in the grips of an idea. She is apparently convinced that all men are conscienceless predators and all women are their helpless prey. What did you see?"

"A folder. A form filled out . . . "

Pottery threw up a hand and closed his eyes. " 'And writes on a pink official form, I do not like my work.' Auden."

"There was also a letter, signed by Amanda Pick. She signed the form, too."

A moment of silence. He might have been observing the death of reason. "Poor girl. How they must have importuned her. The whole sad business goes back to the tenure decision that loomed over her."

"How so?"

"My dear fellow, a permanent place on the faculty is a sinecure. Seats on the stock exchange are less coveted. I have heard the young say that they would kill for tenure."

"Surely that is just a manner of speaking."

"One more tenured member of the department, one less open slot."

"You mean someone junior to Amanda."

"Not necessarily." He widened his eyes significantly. But then he waved the thought away. "Listen, I did not kill the one I love, neither with a kiss nor a sword. Please make a note of that."

"Do you think you will be charged?"

"Of course. 'The lights are going out everywhere, civilization decays, justice disappears, we are left with nothing but lawyers.'"

"And you are innocent?"

"Of what happened to her? Innocent as a babe."

"Amanda's folder makes mention of the fact that you had proposed marriage."

Pottery nodded. "And not as element of any complaint?"

"No."

"Of course not. Well, let them do their worst. I am naked to my enemies."

Not a particularly attractive image, given the girth of the man, and there was something histrionic in the way he professed to welcome adversity. Had love come late but truly to Sean Pottery? If the man would only cut the BS, it might be possible to say. Harvey almost hoped that it was true. As he understood his task, he must do everything he could to limit the damage to the university that might follow on a charge against Pottery. It did not help that Jewel and the office she ran, an official function of the university, would be providing ammunition against Pottery.

"Jewel, what do you have against him?"

"Don't you know?"

He knew that she claimed to have been physically assaulted by Pottery in a public place, namely, the bar of the Morris Inn. She claimed that he had thrown a drink in her face and then accused her of trying to steal it. The bartender had acceded to Pottery's request that the women be thrown out of the bar.

"I would have stayed and fought, but I was soaking wet. The blouse I was wearing was ruined."

"Have you thought of bringing suit?"

"Of course I've thought of it. I consulted a woman lawyer and we went over every detail. She counseled against pursuing it. I had no witnesses. It would have been my word against his."

Harvey brightened. "That was the university counsel?"

"Ha! That woman is an honorary male, a traitor to her sex. She told me to sue if I wanted to, but whether I did or not, I must not speak of what had happened. Particularly if I intended to sue."

Jewel obviously regarded this as hostile advice, but it sounded right to Harvey—if she wanted to make a fool of herself and sue Pottery. Well, she was getting her revenge now. Pottery was doubtless right that it was Jewel who had spread the story of Amanda's sexual harassment charge against him.

Harvey went downtown to the bar of the Jefferson Hotel where brothers and sisters of the press gathered. He bought drinks for an influential few, gave out in dribs and drabs what he hoped would appear in their stories.

"Stories? The *Tribune* has spiked most things written on it."

"I hadn't noticed."

"Believe me."

Of course it was television that mattered. Nobody read anymore, maybe the art was dying out. The nation was become one large, glazed eyeball, fed images from the flickering tube. After four drinks, having done his duty for the university, Harvey returned to his office where a voice mail from Father Finn awaited him. He called.

"I received your report on the donation of Noah Beispiel. Has it been released?"

"It awaits your approval Father."

"Forget it for now. A problem has arisen. The Chesterton short story, which was a condition of the gift, is missing from the archives."

36

Whelan was rendered speechless by the discovery that the Chesterton manuscript of the original Father Brown story was nowhere to be found in the archives. Alone with Roger, he managed to enunciate a sufficient number of words to indicate that the manuscript should be among the *Scholastic* papers. That is where Amanda had discovered it. Something in the way Whelan conveyed this suggested something else to Roger.

"And where you had placed it?"

Whelan nodded vigorously but, with fright in his eye, stopped to look at Roger. Roger patted his arm to reassure him. Whelan must have put the manuscript in Amanda's path, trusting that she would come upon it and realize what it was. And so she had. Roger remembered the excitement with which Amanda had told him of her discovery. Had what seemed then such a stroke of fortune turned into misfortune? It would never be known now what effect it might have had on Amanda's tenure decision.

"You think the missing story has something to do with Amanda's death?" Phil asked.

"That will surely occur to someone."

"Of course it will. What do you make of Noah Beispiel?"

"He is a not an untypical rare book dealer."

"Is that story so valuable that he would pay that much for it?"

"In the nature of things, it can only become more valuable than it now is."

"His gift of papers has the look of a bribe."

"But he is paying for the story."

"Would the university give any consideration to his offer if he weren't about to hand over all those other Henry Horan papers?"

Neither Phil nor Roger was surprised to learn that Roy Gross was fascinated by the missing manuscript's possible connection to his investigation. He appeared at the archives with a search warrant that he did not have to use and left two detectives to consult with Whelan. Meanwhile, a search warrant was served on Pottery in his office, and another at his apartment, and both places were subjected to a thorough examination.

"What are you looking for?"

"Some papers are missing from the archives."

"Of course I have things from the archives here."

"You do?"

"They have been under your nose for the past half hour." Pottery waddled to his desk, moved an ashtray and a pile of books, and pulled two manila folders more fully into view. The two young women fell on the folders avidly, but a minute later sat back. The one whose hair was the color of rusty metal looked reprovingly at Pottery. "These aren't what we're looking for."

"And what would that be?"

She consulted her notebook. "A short story called 'Star of the Sea.' A Father Brown story by Gilbert Chesterton."

"There is no such Chesterton story."

"Well, it's missing."

"I suppose not existing is a species of absence."

The rusty-headed one looked at her companion, whose raven hair had the blue-green highlights of oil in water. Then she said to Pottery, "They had it in the archives and now they can't find it. You're supposed to know more about Chesterton than anyone else."

Pottery bowed. "That is probably true. And on that basis I tell you that you are embarked on a fool's errand. Unless, of course, you are engaged in the investigation of fraud."

Pottery explained to them that no story of the title they mentioned could be found among the authentic Chesterton Father Brown stories, those that had been brought out in four collections during the lifetime of the writer. Admittedly, "Star of the Sea" had a certain plausibility as a title and the text was not without merit, but that was the most that could be said of it.

"Have you actually seen the manuscript?"

"I was shown a photocopy of it. I gave my opinion then."

"That it was fake."

"That it is not genuine."

This, if true, certainly colored what the two detectives were engaged in finding. The assumption was that a valuable manuscript was missing, one for which a considerable sum of money had been offered. "By someone who 'also' claims to know a lot about Chesterton."

"Also?"

"Do you know him?"

"It was your 'also' I queried, ma'am. I made no claim to know a lot about Chesterton. What I did was accept your remark that no one knew more than I did. If someone wishes to offer a large sum of money for an inauthentic story, I suppose there is no statute opposing his folly. But I should think that the university would put itself in a very vulnerable position if it sold as genuine what I have assured them is not."

Noah was in the archives when Roger talked to Whelan about the missing manuscript. The bookdealer had not yet said that, unless he was able to buy "Star of the Sea," his offer to donate the Henry Horan papers to the university was withdrawn. But that, of course, had been the deal. There was little doubt that Noah was unhappy about this turn of events, but he had the air of a man who thought it was a temporary problem susceptible of solution.

"Did Professor Pick ever have possession of the manuscript?" Noah asked.

"S-s-she f-f-found it," Whelan managed to say.

"I realize that. At the time, did she come out here to get you or did she bring the manuscript with her from her workroom?"

Whelan conveyed to Noah that he himself had not been in the archives at the time.

"I was," Roger said. "She showed me the manuscript first, I believe."

"Ah."

"She made a photocopy, of course."

"Of course?"

"Once she had satisfied herself of its genuineness, there was no need for her to work with the manuscript itself."

"Where was the photocopy made."

"I made it," Whelan said. "Here." He pointed at the copying machine that occupied a corner of the room they were in.

"And she never took the manuscript from the archives?" Noah asked.

"N-n-no. Absolutely not." Whelan might have gone on about archive rules and regulations, but he wisely stopped while he was ahead. This excursion into mendacity left him dizzy.

Roger, on the other hand, had fallen silent. After a moment he excused himself and went off down the corridor to the storage room in which the records of the *Scholastic* were kept and where Amanda had made her great discovery. Noah's question had reminded him of the fact that Amanda had shown him the story after they had gone to the Huddle, opening her briefcase so that he could see it. That had been the original manuscript. There was no need to tell Noah this, of course. Like everyone else, he had fallen into the mode of the inquiring detective— when did you last see this, talk to him, etc. The establishment of an exact chronology often provides a list of largely irrelevant items. That Amanda had, in the excitement of her discovery, removed the precious manuscript from the archives, was doubtless a fact. But she had returned it and now she was dead. This was a fact, indeed, but an irrelevant one.

That night, Roger and Phil had dinner at Parisi's, a restaurant from whose windows they could look across Highway 23 and see the unobstructed expanse of the Notre Dame campus. The baseball stadium, the great domes of the Joyce Athletic and Convocation Center, the stadium, the library, the golden dome with the spotlights trained upon it, and in the steeple of Sacred Heart two moonlike faces of the steeple clock, one facing south, the other east. Although Roger did not drink, Phil had ordered a full bottle of red wine, and now they were dawdling at the table while he sipped the final glass. They were still there when Harvey Michaels came in, alerted to where they were by the message Phil had put on the answering machine. Harvey, still wearing his overcoat, sank into a chair he had pulled to the end of the table. He was breathing hard, and he had brought with him the freshness of the wintry night.

"We've got another."

"Another?"

"Body. Laura Flynn has been found dead."

"My God!" Roger cried, and blessed himself.

"Where?"

"At home."

Phil was pushing away from the table, but Roger didn't move. In the distance the great gold statue of the Blessed Mother stood atop the dome of the Main Bulding. "May she rest in peace," Roger murmured. "May she rest in peace."

Harvey nodded. "Amen."

And then they hurried out to the van.

had been flung upon the bed. Her mouth was open, and her sightless eyes stared into space. The scarf still knotted around her neck had choked the life out of her. The medical examiner was already there, and Roger was only able to peek into the room. Then he moved away, shuffling down the hall to another bedroom. He went inside and to the closet, which he opened. He stood for a moment looking at its contents and then closed the door. He went to the kitchen, drawn by the smell of coffee. Harvey and a reporter from the *Tribune* were comparing notes at the kitchen table. Roger took a mug from the cupboard and poured himself a cup of coffee. Harvey said, "You knew where the mugs are."

"I've been here before."

It was difficult not to think of his visits to this house to see Amanda, often to see Laura as well. Two bright and wonderful young women, now both dead. Roger went on to the living room, where he sat on the middle cushion of the couch, held his mug in both hands, and looked around the room. This had been the scene of Sean Pottery's comic declarations to Amanda. Thanks to Jewel Fondue, Pottery had become an object of suspicion on the part of the police for the murder of Amanda. Would this new murder also be laid at his door? Roger found this preposterous. Until a moment later.

From below, there suddenly arose a great roar of protest, scuffling, the sounds of several people on the basement stairway. By the time Roger got to his feet and out of the living room,

Pottery was being propelled upward in the basement stairwell. He was followed by a uniformed policeman wearing a look of professional satisfaction.

"I found this guy downstairs," he announced.

Just as Roy Gross entered the kitchen, Phil with him, Sean Pottery, his clothes in disarray, hair wild on his head, reeking of booze, blinked around the room. "What in hell is going on?"

"What was he doing, Monk?"

The officer answered as if he were giving a report. "I saw him lying on the couch, and my first thought was, it's another body. I turned on the light and didn't see any sign of breath. I could smell alcohol though. I went to the couch and shook his shoulder. He leapt up like a madman and began flailing around. I managed to get him under control and upstairs."

"What are you doing in this house?" Gross asked Pottery.

"What are *you* doing here?"

"Let's take turns, should we? Me first. How long have you been here?"

"What time is it?" He looked around the room, found the clock, closed one eye. "Is that ten o'clock?"

"How long have you been here?"

"I need some water."

There was a den downstairs where Amanda and Laura watched television, alone or separately, the noise not disturbing the house. Sean Pottery had been found asleep on the couch there, an empty scotch bottle beside him. If he had brought it full, its emptiness might provide a gauge of how long he had been in the house. But a significant amount of the liquor had been spilled on the carpet, leading to speculation that Pottery had stopped drinking and fallen asleep after he tipped over the bottle and there was no more to drink. His explanation of his presence in the house was romantic enough to be true.

"I have been keeping vigil," he said. "I just wanted to be here where she had lived."

As nearly as he could remember, he had been there since

late afternoon. How had he gotten there? By cab. The officer called Monk was sent to see if he could verify this. How had Pottery gained entry to the house?

"By the door."

"It was unlocked?"

"I don't have a key."

A tentative time of death was established by the medical examiner. Four or five hours ago. It was now 10:15. When Monk returned with the information that a cab had brought a man to this address at six o'clock, the circle around Pottery closed. He had by now been told why all these people were in the house.

"Was anyone home when you got here, Professor?"

"No one answered when I called out."

"Did you go immediately downstairs?"

"No, no. I looked around up here, I called out, I wanted to be given permission to just sit here awhile."

"Permission from whom?"

"From Laura."

"Did she refuse it?"

Pottery inhaled deeply, then let it out slowly. Several backed away from the fumes. "I did not see her."

"Did you look in the bedroom?"

It was a graceless, clumsy effort but it had aspects of nobility. Pottery rose from his chair and swung at the questioner, but the action had the effect of upsetting his balance and he had to be caught before he fell to the floor. Now that he was up and in hand, he was taken away. Perhaps the police would have been irresponsible not to take Pottery downtown, where they could sober him up and, at the sufferance of his lawyer, question him; but Roger found it impossible to think that Pottery had killed anyone, least of all either or both of these two young women.

Later in the van, when Phil was returning Roger to their apartment prior to going downtown to see what was transpiring with Pottery, Roger said, "Laura had a husband, Phil. An

207

estranged and unhappy man. It would be a good idea to find out where he has been while these things were happening."

Fred Cossette came by early the next morning and he too spoke of Tony Ryan.

"He's been around and I know for a fact that he is a violent man."

Fred told the Knight brothers of the occasion when Tony had shot at him and the circumstances of the attack.

"Obviously he still wanted to think of her as his wife, even though he had gotten their marriage annulled."

"He tried to kill you?"

"Probably not. He was close enough to hit me if he had wanted. He shot out the back windows of my car."

"Did you report this?"

"Laura begged me not to. When I got my car repaired, I said it was a drive-by shooting."

"Have you seen him since?"

"No, but obviously he never left town."

"How do you know that?"

"Look what happened to Laura."

Fred had given the matter a lot of thought. Amanda had been found wearing Laura's jacket. "Tony must have mistaken her for Laura." He rubbed his face with both hands. "If he tried and made that mistake, of course he was going to try again and do it right. And we just sat here waiting for it to happen."

This was a spoor that Phil was inclined to pursue himself; after all, Roger had first suggested it. Phil had made no mention of it at police headquarters the night before, when Pottery waived the right to call a lawyer and had turned his interrogation into a seminar.

"He just sat there lecturing them, Roger."

"It's not a seminar when you lecture."

"Whatever. He professed to find a parallel between recent

208

events and a Father Brown story and went on and on about it. I guess they thought it was his way of coming clean."

"What Father Brown story was it?"

"Not the one that was stolen."

"Oh, Pottery doesn't think that's genuine."

"Isn't it?"

"Yes."

"You're sure?" But Phil took back the question as soon as he asked it. He knew Roger would not make a claim to knowledge if he was not sure.

38

Michaels as if Harvey were personally responsible for the loss of two members of the faculty.

"A scythe is cutting through the ranks," he said, raking his thinning red hair into a wilder condition. "This has to stop!"

A new fund drive was to be announced the following week, and it would not do to have so important an event eclipsed by the investigation into the murders of Amanda Pick and Laura Flynn. That Professor Pottery, one of the most distinguished members of the faculty, was in custody as a suspect only compounded matters.

"Bail him out!" Finn cried.

"He won't let me. He's been there long enough to sober up, and now he is telling the world what an awful person he is."

Pottery's exact words were, "O! what a rogue and peasant slave am I," but there was no need to agitate Finn anymore than he already was. Harvey had begged Pottery to accept freedom and above all to stop talking to reporters, police, and anyone else within earshot.

"I am Boethius in his cell in Pavia, like him, guiltless as charged, but for all that conscious of the rightness of what is happening to me."

Finn wanted to know if he had confessed.

"Should I ask a priest to go see him?"

Finn's eyes narrowed. "I meant confessed to the police."

"Oh, no. He says he is innocent."

"Then why won't he agree to be bailed out?"

Although he professed innocence of any crime, Sean Pottery left open the possibility that he had done dreadful things while drunk. In that case he was guilty of drunkenness and only by derivation guilty of what he may have done while drunk. Such distinctions were not normal jailhouse fare. The police were used to unqualified professions of innocence on the part of those being held. When Pottery began to have memories of encountering someone in the den, of struggling with a mysterious stranger who tipped over a bottle of scotch, frowns formed on the foreheads of Pottery's captors. But they retained Pottery in custody.

A pale, ungainly man with unblinking eyes awaited Harvey when he returned to his office. "Do you remember me?"

Harvey made a show of trying to recall. Had he ever seen this guy before?

"Wiener. Hans Wiener. You did a little piece on me for *Notre Dame Magazine.*"

"Hot Dog Wiener!"

The young man's smile was sepulchral. "I'm up for tenure this year. In the philosophy department."

"But wasn't Amanda Pick up for tenure this year?"

"We both were. That's why I've come to you. My wife and I remembered the nice things you said in that article. It may actually help my cause. But everything is clouded now because of Amanda's death."

His visitor took on a pitiable status. If he regarded Harvey Michaels as his champion, he must be bereft of support indeed. Harvey was beginning to have vague memories of what he had written. Now he recalled sitting in on Wiener's class. Completely unintelligible, but the kids stayed awake. The piece on him had been written in a familiar state of suspended disbelief. Writing about the faculty would tax the creative powers of the most practiced hack. At the outset, Harvey had been unable to do it; but with the passage of years and the disappearance of principle, he now found it easy to dash off a puff piece on a professor. So easy that he retained almost no memory of having done so.

"You made the nickname 'Hot Dog' stick."

Harvey had attributed this to students, though he had never heard it used; but apparently his creative sourcing of his story had conferred on Wiener an epitaph that suggested he was loved by his students. And, of course, students are influenced by the alleged fact that their predecessors liked a given teacher. Harvey was not comfortable in the role of Hans Wiener's benefactor.

"So what can I do for you?" If he expected another story about him, it was best to get it on the table and squash it right away.

"I need your advice."

"Shoot."

Bad word choice. Wiener, who had been leaning toward Harvey like one of those perpetual motion birds, sat back. But then he started to talk and he dipped forward a bit. Harvey felt like putting a glass of water in front of him. The problem, it emerged, was that Wiener thought people suspected him in the deaths of Amanda and Laura.

"Has anyone said that?"

"No! That's what's so awful. But I know they're thinking it."

"Why would they think it?"

"We were in competition for tenure. Only one of us could get it. With her dead, it looks as if I'm a sure bet. You can see . . . "

"Have the police talked to you?"

"What I want to ask is, should I go talk to them?"

"To tell them you didn't kill two women?"

Wiener thought a bit. "That does sound strange."

"It sounds crazy. Look, if they had any reason to suspect you, they would have come to you."

"I almost wish they had."

"Why?"

"Because then the question would be asked and answered and people would know I didn't do it."

213

"Who do you think suspects you?"

"I don't know! That's what makes it so difficult. Maybe Professor Cheval or Quirk."

Wiener had a grip on the arms of his chair, and it was pretty clear to Harvey that the young philosopher had settled in for a long discussion. After half an hour of it, Harvey proposed a solution.

"What we will do is this. You are going to prepare a statement, detailing what you were doing and where at the time of death of Amanda Pick . . ."

"I was up with a sick baby!"

"Good. And Laura Flynn, what you were doing when she was killed. We'll get all that written down. A complete statement. I will have it on file here, and if the police should ever come to you just refer them to me and the statement will take care of things."

"But it isn't the police I'm worried about."

Harvey inhaled. "Okay. So just let people know that you have made a complete statement."

"To you?"

"Just say you've made a complete statement. Let them finish the thought. Obviously, since you're still walking around free, they will conclude that the statement exonerates you."

Wiener was nodding now and his expression was less bleak. "That's a good idea."

"Thank you."

"Shall we get started?"

"No time like the present." Harvey turned to his computer and began to write. From time to time he threw a question at Wiener but kept his eyes on the monitor and his fingers continued to fly over the keyboard. He printed out a copy for Wiener, who read it carefully and slowly. If he criticized it, Harvey would give him the heave-ho. He could not stand amateur critics of the art he knew he had mastered.

"Should I sign it?"

"Do that."

He put the signed statement in a file drawer and then stayed on his feet. He put out his hand to Wiener and the young professor rose reluctantly. He looked at Harvey. "Thank you very much. Teresa was right about you."

"Teresa?"

"My wife. This was her idea."

Harvey was about to ask where Teresa was when Amanda and Laura were killed, but he suppressed it. He had a hunch that Hot Dog Wiener was a little deficient when it came to a sense of humor.

39

husband had set Phil's mind going. A couple of phone calls
to the number listed in the name of Anthony Ryan in
Mankato, Minnesota, that resulted in nothing more than a
recorded message asking him to leave a message after the
beep, prompted Phil to call up on Roger's computer the yellow pages for Mankato and consult the entries under Private
Investigator. There were six. Most of them would earn their
living scaring up evidence for divorce trials or tracking down
runaway children. Well, Phil didn't need a mental giant for
the task he had in mind. More or less randomly he selected
Genevieve Barry and dialed the number. The phone was
answered on the second ring.

"Barry Investigations?"

"Is this Genevieve?"

"Who is asking?"

Phil explained who he was and offered to give her half an
hour to check him out and call him back, but she waived that
and he told her what he wanted done.

"Is that all?"

"I need the information as quickly as possible."

"You'll get it."

Less than two hours later Genevieve Barry called back.
Anthony Ryan was not at home, he had not been seen in
Mankato for over a week, and he was notorious for grousing
about his former wife, whom he described as a radical feminist.

If Anthony wasn't in Mankato, was he in South Bend? That

he had been here recently was clear from what Laura had told Roger. Fred Cossette in turn said that he had been attacked by a man Laura identified as her former husband.

It didn't make much sense that a man who had gone to the extreme of having his marriage to Laura annulled in an ecclesiastical court would be jealously scaring off other men who became interested in her. But the episode with Fred Cossette made it clear that the annulment had not rid Tony of his attachment to his wife. And a man who would shoot out the windows of Fred Cossette's car was capable of violence. If one began with a violently jealous former husband, a complete explanation of recent events was so obvious that the police concentration on Pottery seemed doubly absurd.

Item. The body of Amanda Pick was found clad in a jacket bearing in large letters the legend WOUND. Only Bridget Quirk and Laura owned such jackets. Ergo, Amanda might have been killed under the mistaken impression that she was Laura.

Item. The murder of Laura then appeared to be merely the correction of a mistake. This time the murderer killed the right woman.

Item. In Pottery's drunken, fuddled explanation of his presence in the house when Laura was killed, there had been mention of encountering some mysterious stranger and struggling with him. That his scotch had been spilled all over the floor etched the event in Pottery's memory. It was after that that he fell asleep on the couch in the basement television room. Had that stranger been Tony?

Phil drove himself to the house the two murdered women had shared. The place was taped off and still under investigation so Phil could count on a policemen being on guard who would let him in. When he parked across the street from the house, he saw the patrol car in the driveway, and there were lights on in the house, not in the front rooms, somewhere deeper.

Phil got out of the van, crossed the street, and went up the driveway. He made enough noise to alert the cop on duty that he was coming but not so much as to wake the neighborhood. The driveway ran along the side of the house and brought him to the back door. A light was on in the kitchen. Phil climbed the steps and was about to call out when he saw the man slumped over the kitchen table. A cop. Asleep. Phil smiled, but then the stillness of the slumped-over cop made him wary. Silently, he backed down the steps and got out of the light cast from the kitchen. He stood for a moment in silence and then circled the house on the opposite side. The middle windows on that side of the house glowed mutely, and when he got to them he saw that while there was a light on inside, the shades had been pulled. One shade had not been pulled all the way down. This enabled Phil to see the man in the bedroom, crouched over the open drawer of a desk.

There was a revolver in the van and prudence dictated going to get it. But it was urgency rather than prudence that took Phil back to the kitchen door. He let himself in silently and then heard a moan from the cop, who had pitched forward onto the table. Phil went on past him and into the hallway. From where he stood in the door of the bedroom, the intruder was intent on searching the desk. There was an old army .45 on the bed, perhaps dropped there by the intruder to free his hands.

Phil stepped into the room, picked up the .45, and had just lifted it as the man turned. "What are you looking for?"

"Who the hell are you?"

Phil was suddenly certain that he was facing the man who had killed both Amanda and Laura, the man who had disabled the cop in the kitchen, maybe by hitting him over the head with the .45, and he felt a powerful impulse to do the man harm. The man had only half raised himself from the crouch he had been in to inspect the drawer. The angry expression on his face had been there even before Phil had surprised him and taken possession of his weapon.

"That gun isn't even loaded."

"Then you have nothing to fear."

The man made a break for the door, stiff-arming Phil. But this exposed his ribs, and Phil jammed the barrel of the .45 into his side, once, twice, knocking him down with the second blow. He flipped the man over onto his stomach and dragged first one hand and then the other behind him. Levering one wrist upward along his spine, he raised the man, who was crying out with pain, to his feet. Phil steered him into the kitchen, where the cop looked up groggily and then managed to stagger to his feet.

"Call for help," Phil suggested. "You are about to make an arrest."

"Who is he?"

"The man who hit you over the head, for one thing." Phil fished the billfold out of the man's back pocket and handed it to the cop, who took it and extracted a Minnesota driver's license.

"Ryan" he read. "Anthony Ryan."

PART THREE

LATER

40

tery, Anthony Ryan did not utter a word once Officer Orlowski identified him. He might have been a preconciliar Trappist who had taken a vow of silence. Pottery emerged from jail like Saint Paul being led forth by the angels and held an impromptu news conference on the steps of the courthouse. Asked if he was happy now that justice had prevailed, he cocked an eyebrow and looked with uncharacteristically clear eyes at the questioner. "Justice had nothing to do with it. Mercy has prevailed over justice."

Reporters wrote this down, but he refused to gloss it for them, so it did not appear in any account of the event. But Harvey Michaels saw in the release of Pottery the opportunity to do what he was expected to do, that is, deflect all possible bad publicity from the university. For all too long the campus had seemed an arena of danger and menace. A young professor had been found dead on the jogging path around the lakes, her housemate was found dead in their residence, and to compound matters, a senior professor had been held as a suspect in both deaths, a professor who insisted on broadcasting his plight to the four winds, seemingly exulting in the humiliation brought down on himself and on his university. Now events could be put into a proper perspective.

Harvey settled down to his computer, combed his beard for some minutes with a stubby hand whose nails were bitten to the quick, a meditative glint in his eye. And then his hands descended on the keyboard, and Harvey Michaels wrote the story that would not only become, in a matter of hours, the official version of events, but would also be disseminated far and wide by the media. Harvey wrote of Notre Dame professor Laura Flynn's ex-husband who had come to the South Bend campus to avenge his broken marriage. (No need to bring up the sticky matter of the annulment.) Resentment and rage had been building up in the man, and he arrived at Notre Dame a ticking time bomb of violence. (Harvey repeated the phrase half aloud and found it good.) Stalking his wife, he acquainted himself with her habits, salient among them a morning run around the campus lakes. This provided him with the opportunity to perform his deadly deed.

On a misty morning he lay in wait for her and when she came along he attacked. Her lifeless body was then flung into the lake. Whatever twisted satisfaction the deed gave him was short-lived. The body eventually found in the lake was not that of Laura Flynn but of Amanda Pick, another young professor with whom Laura shared a house. Amanda had gone running that morning and, fatefully, had worn a distinctive jacket that had belonged to Laura. It had not been realized that, from that point on, Laura Flynn was in maximum danger.

The investigation wandered off on tangents. Meanwhile, Anthony Ryan waited to pounce again. Inevitably he did, strangling Laura in her home. And still the true nature of these events was not grasped by the official investigators. Finally, Tony was apprehended in the very house where the second murder had taken place, surprised by a policeman assigned to keep an eye on the house. All in all, an ironic tragedy. The Notre Dame family mourned the loss of two of the most promising members of her faculty and hoped for swift justice to be administered to the outsider who had wrought such havoc on the historic campus.

There are few pleasures like the pride of authorship, and Harvey Michaels, like Browning's "Last Duchess," "too soon made glad," experienced this pleasure every time he sat at his word processor. But this was different in degree, almost in kind. He had the sense that he had dashed off something as memorable as Grantland Rice's legendary likening of the Notre Dame backfield to the Four Horsemen of the Apocalypse. The thought both sobered and inspired. Harvey looked over his prose. He must salt it more with words like "stalk" and "predator." He must stress that the killer was an outsider. A passage teased his mind—scriptural? He could look it up. Something about going about like a roaring lion, seeking something or other, mayhem, wasn't it? He would look it up. The eye that now fell on the screen of the monitor was filled with reverence, almost awe. This could be the piece that made him a legend in the annals of Notre Dame.

Father Finn liked it. He read it immediately when Harvey put it into his hands, nodding.

"Good work."

"It takes the university off the hook."

"Better check that citation from Saint Peter."

"Which one."

Finn glanced at him. "There are so many different translations now, but I've never seen it rendered this way. Use the old version. 'Your adversary the devil like a roaring lion goes about the world seeking whom he might devour.' "

Harvey snapped his fingers, as if his memory had just kicked into the proper groove. "That's much better."

"You know who pulled our chestnuts out of the fire, don't you? Philip Knight. And he was Father Carmody's suggestion. It goes to show you."

What high principle this illustrated Harvey did not know. But he left the associate provost's office with a sense that his own efforts had been insufficiently praised. By the time he got behind the wheel of his car, Harvey was thoroughly deflated. He had been swollen with a craftsman's pride when he'd brought the statement to Finn; now he felt dismissed. And it rankled that his vague memory of the biblical quotation had been corrected. Seated behind the wheel of his car, before starting the motor, he wondered if Finn was right about it. Harvey got out his cellular phone and dialed campus ministry and was answered by a unisex voice.

"This is Harvey Michaels."

A long pause. "Yes."

"Father Finn asked me to check something. Is there a priest there?"

"This is Sister Carmelita. What can I do for you?"

My God. Old Chewy, whose teeth were half bared even in repose. She had short hair and a long memory for even the least of slights. Carmelita had confided to many crowded auditoriums that she felt a call to the priesthood.

"I want a recent translation of a biblical passage." He closed his eyes and gave it as he remembered Finn giving it.

Silence. "Did he give you the exact reference?"

"The Gospel of Peter?"

"I'll look it up. Where can I reach you?"

Harvey rattled off four digits chosen randomly from the series of whole numbers.

"And the name?"

"Fred Cossette."

He hung up. He would have called Theology, but the last time he had asked for help with a quotation there he had gotten a lecture on proof texts from someone named Agenbite. He started the motor and drove without thinking. The horse knows the way. Minutes later he was parked in the lot of the University Club.

41

" 'THE BARGE SHE SAT IN, LIKE A burnished throne, gleamed upon the water,' " Sean Pottery intoned, ensconced at his table in the bar of the Morris Inn. He beamed at the others who'd welcomed him back. Some of them represented a family tradition, being both habitués and sons of habitués, as Pottery had once put it.

"Who wrote that, Professor?" Raoul the bartender asked.

"Don't twit me, Raoul. Bring me a bottle of Perrier."

"Perrier *water?*"

"Water. *Hudor ariston.* I was dragged off into captivity a slave of the senses. I have emerged cleansed and renewed, and so I shall remain."

He kept this resolution for half an hour until a still, small voice told him that beer need not be counted as drink. And if not beer, not wine either. Nor brandy. He ended the evening with brandy, and it was said among regulars in the bar that he had never been in better form. He himself decided that he had been granted what runners call a second wind. But the mention of runners proved to be a sad reminder and soon he was proposing toasts to his fallen colleagues.

"Mine is a broken heart," he confessed. "Offered, it was refused, but the gift once given cannot be taken back. Somewhere along that lakeside path half my soul lies interred."

Such sentiments were toasted with enthusiasm and moist eyes. When Harvey Michaels arrived, having come from the University Club through the tunnel that runs from the Center for Continuing Education to the Morris Inn, there was a heightened, even exalted mood in the bar. At mention of the recent tragic events, Harvey said he was reminded of a passage from Peter. He had the attention of the room, but he looked about him with the expression of one whose mind has just gone blank.

"It doesn't matter," he said lamely, and signaled to Raoul.

"So who *did* kill those women?" Raoul asked.

Harvey's mind cleared and he held forth, giving them the gist of his official statement on recent events.

The flaw in the official university statement was soon pointed out. Amanda Pick had not been killed by the shore of the lake. She had been brought there already dead. But of course it was child's play to handle this wrinkle. Tony had stalked his wife; he knew her schedule and habits. She was an early riser, who started the day with a painful run. He would pounce on her when she emerged from the house. But it was Amanda who rose first that fateful day; and when she left the house wearing Laura's jacket, she was doomed. For some reason, Flynn had then taken her body to the lake and left it in the shallow water near the shore. Had he wished to conceal the mistake he now recognized? Did he return to the house to see if Laura might still be accosted? But she was wakened by the terrible news that Amanda's body had been found by the lake, and by the time she'd dressed and left for the scene below Holy Cross House, Tony, all his plans gang a-gley, was gone.

Meanwhile, Anthony Ryan had made no public statement. Father Carmody went downtown to see if the man wished to speak with a priest and was surprised that he did. Tony got to his feet when the old priest entered and waited for him to be seated. He had a narrow head and deep-set eyes, with something of an El Greco mien. There was a moment of awkwardness, as each waited for the other to begin.

"Is there anything I can bring you, son?"

"I didn't do it, Father."

The priest nodded. He had been warned that the accused always claimed to be innocent. Pottery was only the exception that proved the rule.

"You are a Catholic?"

"I was raised Catholic. We were married in the church."

"What happened there? Wasn't there an annulment?"

"Who told you that?"

"I don't know. Does it matter?"

"There was no annulment."

This obviously meant a great deal to the man. In any case, death had brought to an end his marriage with Laura and not a natural death.

"The letter was forged, Father. I sent her a letter saying the marriage had been annulled. I expected to get a rise out of her. I thought she would object and demand an explanation and then . . . " His voice trailed off. Had he expected a reconciliation once he had gotten her attention in this way?

"Forged?"

"I had written to the marriage tribunal, so I had a piece of their stationery. It was a simple matter to copy the letterhead. That was how I informed Laura that our marriage and been annulled. But she did nothing."

"Did you talk to her after that?"

"She wouldn't see me. She wouldn't talk to me on the phone. All she would say was, 'We've been annulled,' and hang up."

"And you killed her?"

"No!"

"But you were found in the house . . . "

"I was looking for that letter."

"Why?"

The question surprised him and his excitement ebbed. He said almost in a whisper, "I thought it would prove I didn't harm her."

"How?"

He stared across the table at Father Carmody. He was still whispering when he spoke again. "Bless me, Father, for I have sinned."

"You want me to hear your confession?"

He nodded. Father Carmody had brought a stole with him. He took it from his pocket now, a narrow strip of silk, white on one side, purple on the other, put it around his neck, and leaned forward.

"Go ahead."

Tony had not been to confession in five years, he had not been going to mass, he had sought consolations of the flesh with fugitive partners. Father Carmody helped him examine his conscience, going through the capital sins. Tony readily confessed his faults and deficiencies, but there was no mention made of the deaths of Amanda and Laura.

"I guess that's all."

"Are you sure?"

A nod.

"You realize that this confession will be no good if you fail to mention other serious sins on your conscience?"

Tony straightened in his chair and looked at the priest. He seemed about to smile but didn't. "I didn't kill her, Father. I didn't kill Laura or the other woman."

There was nothing Father Carmody could do but give the man absolution. As he said the formula, slowly, deliberately, he looked at the bowed head across the table and when Tony made the sign of the cross, touching his forehead, chest, and left and right shoulders, Father Carmody was convinced that the man had made a full and complete confession.

When he emerged from the visiting room and was greeted by Roy Gross, Father Carmody was about to say something to the detective when he checked himself. He must consider everything that Tony had told him as under the seal. He could not simply pass on to Gross what Tony had said. Would Tony, having unburdened himself to a priest, begin talking with the police? And what would their reaction be to what he said? It was difficult to imagine them doing anything other than dismissing it.

"Everything go all right, Father?"

Father Carmody pursed his lips and widened his eyes and Gross understood immediately. He displayed a palm. "Forget I asked."

filled Sacred Heart Church, bringing out the faculty in force as well as the morbidly curious from far and wide. Still, there was something impersonal in the large gathering, and Roger felt a lingering sadness when he headed for the library afterward. It seemed a reminder of normalcy to find Noah at work in the archives, poring over the contents of a folder that had been fetched for him by Whelan.

"What is he looking at?" Roger asked the archivist in a whisper.

Whelan wrote it out, less in deference to the rule of silence than in distrust of his ability to say it, *Scrip.*

Scrip had been a student literary magazine that flourished in 1930, the year Chesterton visited Notre Dame and gave his two series of lectures in Washington Hall. Henry Horan had been involved with *Scrip* even more than he had with the *Scholastic.* Noah's untroubled continuation of his sojourn at Notre Dame boded well for the fulfillment of his promise to give his Horan papers to the archives. Doubtless he was remaining until the missing manuscript had been recovered. That theft had been eclipsed by the death of Laura Flynn and then the hullabaloo attending the arrest of Sean Pottery and the apprehension of Tony Ryan.

"Parody is a difficult art," Noah said, when he and Roger had adjourned to a bench outside the library for a restorative smoke.

"But it is an art. What would *Ulysses* be without it?"

"When I read Chesterton, I note the tricks and turns that characterize his style, but to duplicate that without simply paraphrasing it—well, I couldn't do it. Not many could."

Noah was referring to the Chesterton write-alike entries that had been published in the *Scholastic*. Roger agreed that no student had come close to the author of the Father Brown stories, included the unpublished one of blessed memory.

"It has to be somewhere," Noah said.

"That is a necessary condition of a physical object."

Noah looked at him in silence, then decided to let the remark go uncommented upon. "Finding it is not high on anyone's agenda, is it?"

"What advice could we give them if it were?"

So they sat on their bench and reviewed the known history of the manuscript. Roger followed the investigative route that had led Noah to the realization that the manuscript that had nagged Henry Horan's conscience throughout his long life was among the few papers he sent to Notre Dame before his death, papers not among those Noah had bought at auction. The latter had included the diary that had set Noah's search in motion.

"The story got here. There is no doubt of that. It is included in the registry of the papers. I mean the title of the story. There is no identification of it as an authentic Chesterton. But was it ever placed in an archival box with the other papers?"

"It was not there when you went through those boxes?" Roger asked.

"No. Was it when you examined them?"

"If it was, it escaped my notice. Of course I would not have given them so thorough an examination. I went through them like a diner anticipating future courses. These were papers I could peruse anytime in the indefinite future."

"How well do you know Whelan?"

"As well as I knew Amanda, I suppose. Or Laura."

Noah shook his head at this reminder of the tragic deaths of the young women. "I guess I thought campuses were immune to such violence."

"Murder is not a daily occurrence here. But tell me what you know of James Huneker."

Noah relit his pipe and held forth for ten minutes. The thesis of his remarks was that it was libelous to see James Gibbons Huneker as a kind of H. L. Mencken. There was little doubt that Noah's was more than a superficial knowledge of Huneker, and as they rose in the elevator to the sixth floor, Roger felt as he had before that Noah had fashioned an interesting and fulfilling life for himself. What might have been dilettantish interests, on the margins of his everyday work, had been turned into his primary concern and his livelihood as well.

Phil was the recipient of all but universal praise for his part in resolving the mystery surrounding the murders of Amanda and Laura. Father Finn conveyed the gratitude of the university at no longer being in the center of such a story. Jewel Fondue dropped Phil a note, thanking him for what he had done for the cause of women at the university and, in a certificate signed by Bridget Quirk, named Phil an honorary member of WOUND.

"An honorary woman," Roger murmured.

"Don't be jealous."

"Will you get a jogging jacket with the acronym on back?"

"She doesn't say."

Harvey Michaels wanted to do a piece on Phil's role in the apprehension of Anthony Ryan, but Phil put a stop to that. He had neither need nor desire for publicity. One of the attractions of Notre Dame was that he could live in obscurity, hidden in the shadow of his enormous younger brother.

"Right now, all I want to do is wipe it all out of my mind and get back to basketball."

Roger remembered the two women in his prayers. He had formed the habit of attending the 11:30 mass in Sacred Heart.

Afterwards, he sat on, looking at the statue of Mary in the niche above the lady chapel behind the main altar. Why did he feel dissatisfied with Tony as the cause of recent events? Almost as dissatisfied as he had been with Pottery? He looked at his watch. He was to meet Pottery for lunch at 12:30.

"I am seeking consolation in Johnsonian wisdom," Pottery announced to Roger and to everyone else in range of his voice, which meant half the tables in the dining room of the Morris Inn. " 'Marriage has many pains, but celibacy has no pleasures.' " He waited for and received appreciative laughter. "Like all well-turned phrases, it is more false than true. The wise have ever sought to sequester the passions rather than work out an arrangement with them. We are better off single, Roger."

"No one looking at either of us would think single covered our case." Roger's three-hundred-plus pounds were rivaled by Pottery's two hundred and seventy-five. "We represent a quarter of a ton of mortal flesh between us."

Pottery roared. "When they tried to get Chesterton into a car and couldn't, a woman suggested that he get in sideways. 'Madam,' he replied, 'I have no sideways.' "

"I know the feeling."

Pottery mellowed after two manhattans, and as he sipped a goblet of red wine became pensive. "Not even Chesterton could have made a plausible plot out of recent events. A supposedly ex-husband mistakenly kills one woman and then manages to kill his wife, as he intended, then conveniently returns to the scene of the crime to be apprehended."

It was this last element of the story that stayed in Roger's mind and seemed incompatible with Tony's guilt. What had he been looking for when Phil surprised him in Laura's bedroom? Unlike the loquacious Pottery, Tony remained mum about what he had done and why.

"I don't understand it, Father," Roger said one day when he sat with Father Carmody in the lounge of Holy Cross House.

"Ah, well."

"What was he looking for?"

Father Carmody lifted his shoulders and looked away. Roger did not feel encouraged to pursue the subject, but he did.

"I have half a mind to get access to the house and go through it."

"Has that been done?"

"Not that I know of. Would you like to come along?"

Father Carmody seemed to have difficulty with the question. "Yes," he said at last. "Yes, I think I can do that."

43

the desk when Roger filled the doorway of Laura's study. The drawer of a file cabinet stood open, and the folders it had contained were stacked on the desk in front of Noah.

"So you haven't found it yet?"

"It?"

"Father Carmody is with me," Roger said, when Noah strained to look around him. "Why do you think it would be here?"

"What brings you here?"

"The thought that this is where you would look for it."

"So you think it's here, too?"

"It?"

Noah smiled. "Wouldn't the two of you be more comfortable if you came all the way in and sat down?" He gestured toward a couch that stood against the wall. Roger crossed over and lowered himself onto it, sighing as he did so.

"You're very thoughtful. Come in, Father Carmody. You remember Noah Beispiel."

"Of course."

"Noah thinks the missing Chesterton manuscript is in this house."

"Do you suppose that is what her former husband was looking for?" Father Carmody asked.

"Oh, no. He was looking for a forgery."

"He killed his wife for a forgery?"

"No." Roger rocked from side to side, getting comfortable on the couch. "Noah killed her. After he killed Amanda."

Noah's only reaction was to smile. "Her husband did it, Roger. The police are holding him. He will go to trial and he will be convicted."

"What purpose would that serve?"

"Justice?"

There was an impatient sound from Father Carmody, who had taken his seat in a straight-back chair and was following the conversation with great attention. Noah's initial awkwardness at being surprised in the house was gone; he was smiling now and while it would have been an exaggeration to say that he was relaxed, his tension lessened as he realized that he confronted nothing more menacing than Roger's some three hundred, not-too-agile pounds and an elderly priest.

"Noah is becoming adept at handling unwelcome interruptions whenever he seeks to ransack this house in search of the missing Chesterton manuscript." Roger adopted a cheerful narrative tone as he addressed himself to Father Carmody. "Pottery was pummeled for his pains when he showed up here during a previous foray by Noah." Roger turned back to Noah and looked sadly at him. "Laura fared somewhat more tragically on that occasion. Why did you have to kill her?"

Noah turned the question over in his mind. "If you really believed me capable of such a deed, you would not put yourself and Father Carmody in jeopardy by accusing me of it."

"Oh, we are in no danger."

Father Carmody seemed to take comfort from this. He moved to the couch and Roger edged toward the end to make room for him, hoping that this would not have a teeter-totter effect and catapult Father Carmody across the room.

"You're armed?"

"In a sense. I have what you want."

"You do?"

"And you will not find it here."

240

"I believe that is called a bluff, Roger." A memory troubled Noah and he looked away. "Laura tried the same trick. It was when I found it was a trick that . . . " But he stopped. "I suppose I couldn't presume on Father Carmody's clerical status in making what might be construed as a confession. No? That's a pity. Where is the manuscript, Roger?"

"Before we discuss that, you must permit Father Carmody to leave."

Noah tipped his head to one side and looked sadly at Roger. "Let us at least respect one another's intelligence."

"You have made that difficult, Noah. Look at the trail you have left behind you, yet you still are no closer to obtaining the prize that brought you to campus than you were the day you arrived."

"Where is it?"

"Think of what you have done. You were surprised by Amanda, too, I suppose. Poor Amanda has been thought to have been a case of mistaken identity, but of course that wasn't true, was it? She recognized you and must have realized at once why you were in this house. Why did you take her away? Why did you put Laura's jacket on Amanda? Noah, why did you go to such lengths to cover up the first murder you committed in this house?"

"Where is the story?"

"Where it has been since Laura returned it to the archives."

"It is not *in* the archives."

"Can you think of a better place to hide a tree than in the forest."

" 'The Invisible Man.' " Noah mentioned the Father Brown story that turns on the omnipresent invisibility of the mailman.

Roger nodded. " 'The dog that did not bark.' But Chesterton had a proprietary right to the idea that the ordinary constitutes the greatest mystery of all. The manuscript is on my desk in the archives."

"*Your* desk?"

"The table in Whelan's office where I am permitted to work."

It was clear from Noah's expression that he had not looked for the missing manuscript there. But all he did was nod. "Ingenious. A more complicated lie would be easier to dismiss."

"Oh, I am telling the simple truth. Whelan and I agreed to take the manuscript out of circulation, so to speak."

"Why?"

Roger looked abject. "Because of an idea I foolishly set aside. It had occurred to me that Amanda's death might have some connection to her discovery of the Chesterton manuscript. But events made that seem unlikely, events that you arranged."

"How can I be sure you are not lying?"

"Sure? Well, one way would be to go fetch the manuscript."

"The three of us?"

"I suppose that is the only way."

"And after?"

"You can lock Father Carmody and me into the archives. There isn't much point in adding to your troubles by harming us. My brother, Phil, will soon be reading a voice message in which I lay out for him the suspicions that took their final form when Father Carmody and I arrived here and saw that there was somebody in the house."

Noah was on his feet. The thought that Philip Knight would soon be alerted as to where he was and why erased all traces of insouciance, and he became crisply efficient.

"Let's go."

But Roger remained seated on the couch. "You could be a sport about it and let Father Carmody stay here."

"We're all going!"

"Noah, all you can buy is a little time. I suppose you could tie Father up sufficiently so he could not sound the alarm before I come back for him afterward."

"Your insurance policy?"

242

Roger beamed. "In a way. Call it a *pari mutuel*."

Noah hesitated but Roger got to his feet. "I suggest we take my van."

"Sit down!"

Roger sat. But it was not indecision that caused Noah to reverse field. He held up a hand, his head cocked. Roger, too, had heard the sound, but it would have been beyond the diminished range of Father Carmody's hearing. The old priest had half risen from the couch but now settled back again. Outside in the distance there was the sound of a car door closing. An ordinary sound, to be sure, but this was clearly one that was unsuccessfully muffled. Noah removed from his pocket in a swift motion what proved to be a rifle. He snapped the barrel onto the stock and held it out from his body. On guard. It was a cruel weapon, wonderfully engineered to cause harm. Roger had the sudden certainty that he was looking at the weapon used on Amanda and Laura, but as a blunt instrument.

"You dallied too long," Roger said, and Noah whirled on him, pointing the rifle at his rather unmissable target. Did he have any intention of using that weapon then? No matter. The shot that was fired was not by Noah. The rifle spun out of his hands, and the force of a bullet striking his shoulder knocked him off balance. He was sprawled on the floor, stunned and bleeding, when Philip and Roy Gross entered the room. Earl Sanders scooped up the rifle, and Phil looked at Father Carmody and Roger. "What are you two doing here?"

"Thank God you got my message," Roger said.

"What message?"

The two brothers stared at one another. Roger smiled. "There are many ways of communicating. I will wager that Father Carmody has been praying for our safe deliverance."

Noah was strangely docile in Gross's custody, but then he was disarmed now. Noah's pensive look suggested that he was already thinking ahead, searching for his next possible move in the game. But he had been checkmated at last.

EPILOGUE:
AFTERWARD

SUGGESTIONS THAT THE UNIVERSITY sell publishing rights to "Star of the Sea" and then raise more money by the sale of the original manuscript were not welcome in the archives nor, it soon transpired, in the administration. Champions of these venal schemes beat a retreat, explaining that their intention had been that any funds realized should underwrite an appropriate memorial to the two young women who had died because of the manuscript. Such a memorial did not depend on selling such a treasure as a Chesterton holograph. Father Finn made arrangements to have the story—and a flattering version of the story—featured in the profile of Notre Dame shown on national television during halftime of football games. Harvey Michaels was at work on the script and spoke of it as his greatest challenge.

"Will Noah figure in the script?" Roger asked.

"Not even as a footnote."

"I suppose that is the fate of most of us, so far as history goes."

Harvey nodded. "It gives me a sense of power."

Roger let it go. Perhaps serious history is only slightly more evanescent than the products of Harvey's pen.

Sean Pottery rose to new heights of vinous declamation as he regaled the other denizens of the Morris Inn bar with tales of his incarceration. He became in the telling the shoemaker of *A Tale of Two Cities*, Admiral Denton as prisoner of war, and, of course, Boethius in his cell in Pavia. He was thinking of writing of his travails.

"The Consolation of Chesterton?" Roger asked,

Sean Pottery shook his leonine head. "No. My interest in Chesterton has been a casualty of these events, Roger. How could I read him now without being reminded . . . " His voice broke and trailed off. "I was thinking of poetry."

"Prison literature?"

"Indeed, indeed. Fr. Leo Ward turned to verse in his twilight years."

At Notre Dame, there seemed to be a precedent for everything.

Tony returned to Mankato to take up again the task of teaching. Hans Wiener was granted tenure, an event somewhat eclipsed by the discovery that Teresa was expecting another set of twins. Fred Cossette was seen often in Jewel Fondue's office. What began as a common need to review what had happened became a habit of getting together. All men are beasts, of course; but music soothes the savage breast, and Jewel had Mozart as background Muzak during what can only be called their trysts. Bridget Quirk openly snubbed Jewel in the University Club.

"Time heals all wounds," Roger observed.

Phil, who was an honorary member of the group, was glad to hear it.

In the spring, sometimes alone, sometimes with Father Carmody, Roger visited Cedar Grove Cemetery and stopped at Laura's grave. But his thoughts were of Amanda too, interred in far-off California. Sometimes Father Carmody said a prayer, in Latin. Once they brought Father Rush along. Cemeteries in Bangladesh are very different, he informed them, not at all like this. When he joined in the prayer for the dead, he doubtless thought of those long-ago parishioners of his who had gone on before him. *Requiescant in pace.* May Amanda and Laura rest in peace. Which is a way, Roger thought, of praying for the only tenure that really matters.

THERE IS A WILLOW THAT GROWS aslant Saint Mary's lake on its northwestern shore where the path passes beneath Fatima Retreat House. An elderly figure sat on a bench beside the path surrounded by ducks, to whom he was doling out bits of bread. The ducks were always indiscriminate in waddling toward dispensers of food but this morning, after a first unseasonable snowfall, they would willingly have been fed by a butcher. But the old priest ignored that, preferring to think of himself as Saint Francis, who could charm the birds from the trees and talk to animals in their own languages.

"*Venite ad me omnes,*" he murmured, on the chance these ducks spoke Latin.

There was a lesson to be learned from the mindless greed with which the ducks responded to sense appetite. Only man must subsume his natural desire for food and drink under the governance of reason. It was a lesson Father James had taught in a lesser college of the Congregation for years, but of late he had been assigned to Fatima Retreat House as a preacher of retreats.

Mid-October was a slack time for retreats, and the snow brought thoughts of Christmas and the weeks when the house would be empty and he need think only of his own soul. The creche would remain in chapel long after Epiphany and the smell of pine would perfume his prayers. And, of course, the students would be gone on vacation and the campus, too, all but empty. But this morning's snow was already beginning to melt and soon autumn would be back in full force.

When the bread was gone, the ducks continued to crowd around. He showed them that the bag was empty but they remained. He had neglected to say grace on their behalf before feeding them and said it now.

"Benedic nos, domine, et haec tua dona . . ."

The ducks began to go quacking off to the lake. Perhaps they spoke French or Italian. The priest flattened and folded the empty bag and put it into the pocket of his coat. He rose from the bench. It was time for exercise. He started along the path in a westerly direction, moving slowly. He did not really believe in exercise. Exercise was a poor substitute for genuine labor in a generation gone soft with luxury. He smiled way the thought. He was Francis, not Jeremiah.

This thought was reenforced when half a dozen ducks accompanied him along the path. Clearly they were not land animals, only imperfectly amphibian. But their pace suited his. He was in no hurry. From time to time he stopped and looked back the way he had come, at the spire of Sacred Heart, at the great golden dome of the Main Building. Once, Father Sorin's eyes had rested on them. He felt a profound solidarity with the founder of the Congregation in which he had labored for some forty years.

When he turned he found that his escort of ducks had continued up the path. One had wandered from it and was seeking to conceal what it had found. But the other ducks were not deceived. They waddled across the snow and soon there was a quacking contest for the prize. Father James wondered vaguely what it could be? What foodstuff could they have come upon?

When he reached the point on the path from which they had set off to the quarrel, he stopped again to look benignly at his feathered friends. What they were fighting over seem feathered, too. His curiosity, usually dormant, was piqued. He went across the snow and found that they were playing tug of war with what looked like an Indian headdress. And then he saw the body.

The man was all but covered with snow and there were now many duck tracks around the body. Father James hurried forward and knelt before saying the formula of absolution over the man. Who knew how long the soul would take to leave a frozen body? The back of the head was exposed now that the headdress had been removed. Masses of blood had blackened and frozen in the matted hair. Father James struggled to his feet and as he returned to the path he shooed the ducks before him. Stupid beasts.

And then he went on, in what an undemanding observer might have described as a jog, back to the house to spread the alarm.

The trouble began on an October Saturday at the log chapel.

Two stretch limos came up the road behind Bond Hall, which housed the architecture department, and parked. Out of them poured a wedding party. The bride wore a traditional white gown, the bridesmaids were in blue, the men in formal attire. The groom was an alumnus, the bride his childhood sweetheart, and he was fulfilling an undergraduate dream of being married in the log chapel on the Notre Dame campus, a venue in even more demand than Sacred Heart Basilica, the university church. Father Burnside, who had been rector of the groom's undergraduate dorm, was to meet them at the chapel door.

But there was no sign of the priest.

The chapel door was guarded by two men done up in traditional Indian garb.

"Have you seen a priest?"

"He's inside."

They did not get out of the way. The best man, another alumnus, had made the football team as a student, a tight end who had played a total of eight minutes in a game that had been won already in the first half. He stepped forward, expanded his chest, and explained that a wedding was scheduled.

"The priest is our prisoner, "one of the Native Americans said. "We are reclaiming our property."

In Cedar Grove Cemetery, the sexton was appalled, the more so because he had not noticed the outrage when he came to work that morning, though he must have driven right past the toppled grave markers. One had stood six feet tall and when it fell had done damage to a number of neighboring graves. The sexton called for his crew to make a thorough reconnaissance to see if there were other instances of vandalism.

He assumed that it *was* vandalism, kids from town in the momentary grip of adolescent madness who had thought pushing over gravestones made some profound statement to the universe. There were three desecrated graves, if that was not too heightened a way of putting it. The sexton did not think so. He used the term five times in speaking to campus security. To the provost he spoke of sacrilege.

Cedar Grove Cemetery was as old as the university itself. It was located on Notre Dame Avenue, as good as on the campus,. just south of the bookstore and Eck Alumni Center. For some years there had not be a single unspoken-for grave site in Cedar Grove, but more land had been acquired to the west when the golf course was relocated and now a fortunate few more could look forward to awaiting the last trump in the company of the earliest generation of South Bend.

It was Roger Knight, the Huneker Professor of Catholic Studies, who later noticed a pattern in the vandalism.

Coquillard, Pokagon, Pokagon's son.

Old Father Carmody nodded. "Contemporaries of Father Sorin." Edward Sorin was the founder of the University of Notre Dame, a visionary French priest of the Congregation of Holy Cross who had found a small trading community on a bend in the Saint Joseph River when he came to claim the property he had bought for what he grandly called his university. "French-men like himself," Carmody added.

"Not entirely, Father. Some of them had Indian blood as well. And Pokagon was a chief."

Meanwhile, Father Burnside had been released from custody and the wedding in the log chapel went on as planned. But when the happy couple and their party walked to their rented vehicles to be driven away to the Morris Inn for the reception they had to pass between ragged rows of half a dozen surly men all dressed up as Indians.

"What's going on?"

"Keno sabe?"

"Be careful."

On the following day, Wednesday, the university chancellor did not return as scheduled from a trip to Hong Kong. A call to the Michiana Airport revealed that he had arrived in South Bend on the appropriate flight.

"Johnny!" said Miss Trafficant impatiently. Anita Trafficant was the chancellor's secretary and Johnny the chancellor's driver. There was enmity between her and Johnny. The chauffeur had an annoying habit of acting as if he worked directly for the chancellor and was on an equal footing with Miss Trafficant! She would not have been human if she did not relish the thought of scolding him for whatever had happened. But he did not answer his car phone.

Miss Trafficant believed in scheduling. Her success at her job depended in large part on the efficient way in which she arranged the chancellor's day. Without her precise allocation of his time, he could not have done half of what he did. She had allowed an hour and a half from the time of his arrival at the airport to the first appointment of the day. Father Bloom should be well rested from his long flight in business class across the Pacific.

Two hours passed and the chancellor had not arrived on campus or come to his office. The tenth call to Johnny's car got an answer. His speech was slurred and he made little sense.

"Have you been drinking?"

The answering obscenity was sufficiently garbled that she could honorably ignore it. She managed to learn where he was.

"You were supposed to pick up Father."

There was a call on her other phone. She cut off Johnny and took the call.

"This is the Blue Cloud Nation. The chancellor of Notre Dame is our prisoner. Stand by for further instructions."

The phone went dead.

The consensus in the lounge of Corby, the building where lived priests who were not rectors of residence halls, was that it was a student prank. Johnny had been slipped a mickey and the students who met the chancellor's plane hit upon the politically incorrect excuse that Indians had kidnapped him in an effort to reclaim the property on which the university stood. True, this theory had been floated recently in an allegedly humorous column in the student newspaper, but then it was difficult to distinguish intended from unintended humor in that publication.

"They got the idea from the log chapel incident."

"Or the vandalism in Cedar Grove."

"What if they're all connected?"

"How?"

The speaker had held up one hand as he spoke, but then immediately let it drop to the arm of his chair.

In the faculty senate the Quinlan Resolution was being debated. If passed, it would become the sense of the senate that the administration should appoint a committee to meet with the Blue Cloud Nation in order to review with utmost seriousness their claim that ancestors had been bilked out of the land on which Notre Dame stood.

"It doesn't matter," one phlegmatic senator observed. "There isn't a patch of earth that was not at one time inhabited by someone other than those currently inhabiting it."

"These people weren't even alive at the time."

"Their quarrel is with Sorin."

"He's dead."

"So are their ancestors."

"It's a matter of justice."

"You want to give the place back to the Indians?"

"If they'll have it."

"If it is theirs it would not be a gift."

An observer from the *Observer* thought that the senate as a body was inclined to think that Notre Dame had been built on a foundation of injustice and crime.

A video of the captive chancellor was delivered to Corby Hall. He looked disheveled and unfocused, but then he wasn't wearing his glasses. He seemed to be reciting when he spoke.

"I have pledged to correct any injustice that has been done against the Blue Cloud Nation by the University of Notre Dame."

His eyes lifted to the camera and filled with tears. His lower lip trembled. "I'm sorry," he said.

"He didn't know what he was saying."

"So what's new?"

"He was just reading words written for him."

"So what's new?"

"You can't just wish away an institution that has been situated on this land for over a century and a half. What would the Indians do with the land?"

"A casino?"

"They'd sell it."

"That's the answer! Give it back to them and then we buy it right back. If all they want is money . . ."

This turned out not to be true. They wanted the land. They wanted the lakes. They wanted the woodland. They wanted their old burial ground back.

"Where is it?"

"It has yet to be located."

In a conference room in Decio a few days before the trouble began, the graduate committee of the history department was in session. The first order of business was the fate of Orion Plant, a doctoral candidate.

"We've already extended him two times."

"Who's his director?"

Professor Otto Ranke raised his hand but not his eyes. He had lied for Plant too many times and he was not inclined to do so again. The inevitable question was asked.

"Has he made progress on his dissertation?"

"No."

"Is there any reason why the rule should not be applied?" The rule was that a doctoral candidate must submit his dissertation for reading and defense within seven years of getting approval of his topic. Plant's dissertation had been approved eleven years ago. Ranke was not only the director, he was the only survivor of the original committee. All the others were retired or dead. Or both.

"The rule should have been applied earlier."

A vote was taken. The decision was unanimous. Sencil, the director of graduate studies, said he would convey the decision to Plant, but Ranke said that task must be his. The others might rightly feel that they had condemned someone in absentia. Had they even known Plant? Ranke felt that he had just bade adieu to his golden years. Plant was the last candidate who had sought to do a dissertation under his direction.

"What was the topic anyway?"

"The relocation of Indians to the southwest."

The love of learning takes many forms. In some, it is a pure gemlike flame that warms and does not consume the student. In others, it is a means to ameliorate the human condition, first of all in their own case. In a few, as for Nietzsche, it is a path to power for whom knowledge becomes a weapon. A blunt weapon in the case of science, a remote and transcendental one in the case of philosophy, but subtle and sure in the case of history. From the outset, Orion Plant had seen history as revenge upon the present.

As a boy in Toledo he had spent hot summer afternoons in the attic of his grandmother's home, turning over the pages of old albums and ledgers, pondering the facts entered on the flyleaves of old family bibles. He was fascinated, a question grew in him, he followed the spoor of possibility. It was there in the attic with lungs filled with dusty air and sweat running down his broad freckled face, that he had discovered he was not his parents' child. His family was not his family. He had not even been legally adopted. His apparent parents had taken him in when a neighbor went on a trip. The neighbor never returned. With time, the family gave Orion their name and neglected to tell him he was not one of their own. After a moment of vertigo and a pang of sadness, Orion found the discovery oddly exhilarating. What he would learn to call research was a means of overturning the apparently real world.

Acquiring the academic credentials to pursue the surprising secrets of the recorded past as a lifetime task turned out to be more demanding and less interesting than Orion had supposed. But he persisted. He got an undergraduate degree at a small college in his native state and was then admitted to graduate studies at the University of Notre Dame. When he left

Toledo he metaphorically shook its dust from his sandals. At Notre Dame he took with diminishing interest the required number of courses. Availing himself of the unofficial archives kept by generations of graduate students in history, he passed the written and oral examinations and was admitted as a candidate for the doctorate. Resentfully prowling through the past of the area, he chose a topic and it was approved. Professor Ranke nodded sagely through clouds of the sweet smoke rising from his pipe. Orion would chronicle the forced march of local Indians to Kansas just prior to the founding of Notre Dame. He would focus on the martyred devotion of Father Petit, who had accompanied the Indians on their death march. The benign official version of the transfer of the land to Father Sorin invited skepticism.

"He's buried in the crypt of Sacred Heart." Ranke sent up his words in little puffs of smoke. Orion looked at his director impassively. He had nodded through the professor's boring lectures, but now his estimate of his guide sank further. Orion had found the burial plot of Father Edward Sorin in the community cemetery located just off the road that led from the grotto to the highway across which stood Saint Mary's College, the sister institution of Notre Dame.

"Father Sorin?" The question was meant to make Ranke's ignorance explicit.

"No, no. Petit."

"Ah."

Orion thought Ranke might be wrong at least in this, but he was not. This oddly increased his disguised contempt for his director. He began his research.

He had been at it three years when he met Marcia. She worked in the Huddle, preparing stir-fried concoctions to order. He might not have noticed her if she had not, surreptitiously but making sure he noticed, put a double portion of chicken in his order as she began to cook it. The second time this happened he read the name on the plastic badge she wore.

"Marcia."

"Marcia Younger."

"Than what?"

Her pained expression told him he was not the first to make a bad joke of her name.

"I'm sorry."

"Everybody does it."

"I'm Orion Plant."

"I know."

Those behind him in the line were beginning to mutter, but Marcia was practiced in antagonizing customers. He pushed on, paid, and took a table. Some minutes later, minus the plastic snood she wore over her hair while stir-frying, Marcia joined him.

"I asked who you were, that's how I know."

And so it began. She was a substantial young woman but her face was pretty, made even prettier by the adoring expression in her eyes. He was not used to the deference she showed him. She had the impression that he was a junior member of the faculty. As a graduate assistant, he was part of the platoon of indentured servants who made life even easier for the faculty. He felt that he was monitoring the professor's lectures and in his discussion sessions he subtly corrected what Ranke had said. He did not correct Marcia's misapprehension. After all, in a few years . . .

Her father was dead, her mother stone deaf; Orion became a constant visitor in their small house just east of the campus, within walking distance of graduate student housing on Bulla Road. As they walked back from her house they could see Hesburgh Library lift like a great sarcophagus among the trees. It was there that his study carrel was located. After a few months, they seemed to be engaged. When, given her passionate yielding, an early marriage seemed advisable, Orion told her they would be married in the log chapel.

"I'm not Catholic."

259

"That doesn't matter." In his cluttered, imperfectly formed Catholic mind a cunning thought occurred. Marriage to Marcia might not really count so far as the great book in the sky was concerned. He changed his mind about the log chapel, citing as reason his great reluctance that he might be married among those primitive paintings in which the natives obsequiously received the great white fathers. Orion and Marcia were married in the courthouse by a judge who had just sentenced a man to life imprisonment. Orion did not voice the joke that occurred to him. They honeymooned in Niles and moved in with her mother. Marcia wrote down the good news for her mother to read after several shouted versions failed to get through to her staring, open-mouthed parent.

Her father had been in real estate as had his father before him, the family business going back generations. The records of the now-defunct enterprise were in old wooden file cabinets stored in a rental locker north of town. An hour spent perusing them piqued his interest and Orion brought the records to the house and it was not long before his passion for research was diverted to the records of Younger Real Estate. The records went back into the nineteenth century and proved to be a vein of precious ore.

When Roger Knight had accepted the offer of the Huneker Chair of Catholic studies, his brother Philip, a private detective, moved to South Bend with him. For Roger, Notre Dame might be second only to Bardstown, Kentucky, in the American past of the church to which he had converted while a precocious graduate student at Princeton, but for Philip it was a place where seasons of sports succeeded one another liturgically. He continued to conduct his business, though more and more sporadically, from their new location. Roger had earned his doctorate *summa cum laude* at the age of nineteen, a boy who had inflated to dirigible size in the course of his accelerated studies. Armed with his degree he had emerged into a professional world that eyed him with wary caution. He had been on the short list for several teaching positions but in the end was given, in Philip's phrase, the short end of the stick. He lost interest in poring over *The Chronicle of Higher Education* for other opportunities and eventually, when Philip retreated from his Manhattan location to the comparative civility of Rye, Roger applied for and received a private investigator's license and Philip's advertisement in the Yellow Pages of strategically chosen major cities announced that Knight Brothers Investigations could be reached at the 800 number listed. Roger created a web page as well and for some years they had taken on clients with a problem interesting enough to lure them from Rye. Meanwhile, Roger read and communicated via e-mail with kindred spirits about the globe on the myriad of things that engaged his scholarly mind. He wrote a book on Frederick Rolfe, aka Baron Corvo, which enjoyed first a *succès d'estime* and then, thanks to its selection by the History Book Club and its adoption by Barnes and Noble, enjoyed a wide readership as well. It was this book that caught the attention of Father Carmody and led to the offer of the Huneker chair.

At Notre Dame, Roger was a free variable floating over departmental divisions. He taught but one course a semester and it was cross-listed in English, philosophy, theology, and history. It was thanks to the latter connection that he had come to know Otto Ranke, an elderly professor to whom the concept of retirement was anathema. To Roger he represented a Notre Dame that was no more, a remnant of the small band whose teaching and writing bore the stamp of the religious affiliation of the university. Now Notre Dame described itself as a national research university and its distinctiveness as an institution, academically at least, was threatened. Today, Otto Ranke, with his interests in the role of the American bishops at Vatican II, and a monograph on distinguished visitors to the South Bend campus that had featured F. Marion Crawford, Robert Hugh

Benson, Henry James, and William Butler Yeats, would have been an unlikely prospect for a position in the history department. With the retirement of Marvin O'Connell and Philip Gleason, Ranke was the history department for Roger Knight.

"A student of mine is writing his dissertation on that," Ranke said one day when they were discussing the past of the coordinates of space the university occupied, and the fate of the Indians had come up.

"I'd like to meet him."

"No, you wouldn't."

"Why?"

"An odd fellow."

Roger would have thought this would be a commendation rather than the reverse for Professor Ranke, but no further explanation was offered. They sat for a moment in silence, enveloped in the smoke from Otto's pipe. The smoke, from irresistible sweetness turned over time into something approaching the American pronunciation of the professor's family name, and there were complaints from purists along the corridor of Decio Hall. Notre Dame was a listed as a smoke-free campus, something that Ranke considered the result of the guttering of the fire of proud and confident Catholicity among the faculty. But he had been here before most of the campus buildings went up, his colleagues' parents had been children when he joined the faculty, and he was unmoved by their reiterated complaints. Smoking was still grudgingly permitted in the faculty office building, but plaintiffs insisted that cigars and pipes were excluded. They had no case. If Ranke noticed that he had been ostracized as an inconsiderate old bastard devoid of sensitivity, he gave no sign of it, but serenely lighted pipe full after pipe full of his aromatic offering to a better day.

Their conversation turned to the recent events in Cedar Grove Cemetery. Ranke nodded as if it too were an expected consequence of the university's swerve into secularization.

"Bigots," he opined, and began to speak of past episodes, notably the depredations of the KKK.

"Religion doesn't seem to be at the bottom if it," Roger said.

"Religion is at the bottom of everything."

Nothing could have stated more succinctly Roger's own conviction and he settled back contentedly to Ranke's impromptu lecture on the hooded hordes that had once harassed the campus.